Animals I've Neglected to Mention

by Jane Wodening

Each story complete and unabridged, written and selected by Jane Wodening.

Some of these stories have been published before. Some have been published before but have been enlarged by the author, most notably *Rosco* from The Inside Story, and *The Captain of the Mice* which was *Living With Mice* in Living Up There. *Mighty Mouse* has been published in World Picture Magazine #13, Summer, 2018.

Published by:
Sockwood Press
P. O Box 706
Nederland, CO 80466

ISBN 978-1-944572-08-2
Library of Congress Control Number: 2019933286

1st edition

A thousand thanks to Betsy Buck, Paul Wallace Thompson , Lucy Strook, Jane Shepard, Normandie Rainwater, Crystal Brakhage, Julian Taylor and Janette Taylor for their brilliant help in pulling this book into shape.

"Everybody is somebody. Even bugs."
— Jane Wodening

INTRODUCTION

Always I've been with animals, if not in my household, then I would find them – in the alley, under a rock, in the field, in someone else's yard, in the trees. Or I'd be thinking about them; they were just there in my mind. The people were authority figures and I learned how to be quiet and let them do the talking. With animals, I always had equality. I respected them and they respected me. Why this didn't happen to other children, I have never learned, except that my parents wanted my brother and me to learn to think for our own selves, although I seem to have always had a basic submissive style.

Naturally, much of my writing is of animals. I've never been interested in writing fiction, although the tale in <u>Wolf Dictionary</u> is partly taken from books by scientists, partly made up, of course, to show the animals expressing themselves in the wild. I've written two memoirs, <u>Driveabout</u> and <u>Living Up There</u>, and both have animals here and there. Many of my animal stories went into the short story collection, <u>The Lady Orangutan and Other Stories</u>, fifty-seven tales drawn from across a lifetime, quite a few of them are of animals.

I remember when I was facing my fortieth birthday, I realized that if I was going to do anything with my life, I'd better get at it. I had begun to write serious stories and I knew what to do. Now, I'm in my eighties and a similar thought occurs to me. Several animal stories important to me have been left at the wayside. A few entries copied out from an old diary show glimpses of animals that I may not have felt able to follow up on. And some I did follow up. Coolie the grackle was one. I had written a story about Tree the goat when she died, but had left out a long life and felt like telling it. She was a great lady and a dear friend.

Stimulus is necessary for inspiration. Many people can write without inspiration, but I don't seem to be able to. Thus, I have written much less than they have.

I never dreamed of being a writer. That would be silly; I could hardly converse. Oh, it wasn't a mental deficiency, nor a lack of education either, although I dropped out of college early in my second year. Zoology lab in my first year was very exciting but I got a C+ as my only comment from the teacher to me. It seemed that although I had hurled myself into Zoology, I wasn't welcomed, wasn't suitable, somehow, and besides, in the Zoology lab, I did nothing but draw the insides of dead animals. This was fascinating and educational but I didn't want to be a veterinarian. If I had heard of Konrad Lorenz and the beginnings of animal behavior studies, at that time, I don't know what I would have done. I went into engineering math but I found logarithms so boring.

Because the story of Coolie the grackle couldn't be finished when The Lady Orangutan and other Stories was ready to go to press, and there was Mighty Mouse waiting in the wings, so to speak, and also the story of the rabbits, I realized I should give fuller perspectives on Rosco and Tree. I needed to show the complexity of the lives of mice. I hunted for other creatures that I had not given the attention I felt they deserved, or stories that simply needed more work so that what I was saying was clear.

Some of the stories I have hesitated to publish because they might be scary or unpleasant; "Sparkle and the Mice" is one, and of course "Critter Suicides" even "Small Animals." But I include them particularly because they portray what I consider important information that our species could actually profit by understanding and applying the understanding of these truths to the shaping of our own culture.

I found quite a number of brief studies and images from an old diary. I collected everything I had ever written about animals, but then it seemed like a hundred animals in a bag. It was huge and ungainly. I removed from the manuscript I was collecting well over a hundred pages of stories that I loved but that had been published at some time in the last eighteen years. But removing the recently published tales made the book seem

too small, and I sat for many weeks, not
finding impetus.

Until one day I found an owl standing on the
ground, staring at me through the wire fence I
put up to keep the chickens out of the
vegetables. I knelt and stared back at him, a
foot away. I felt honored by his visit, wrote it
up as "Owl in the Garden" and put it in the
book, then realized that I hadn't ever written
about the bats and wrote that one. I could also
write that story the guy told me on the bus
about the pig he had when he was a child.
And others came to mind, encounters I had
had but hadn't written up. Now the book
seems complete and I feel a deep gratitude to
that owl for bringing me this gift.

- Jane Wodening, May 30, 2018

X

Table of Contents

Although I didn't write it until decades later, the one story besides "Transformations" (which appears in The Lady Orangutan and Other Stories) that refers to my childhood is the story of Wagsy, and so it seems proper to start with it. If Wagsy had not been obliged to be always on a chain, he might have been a fine little dog. But he was such a gift to me. Without him there on his chain, I don't know what I would have done. He guided me through an important section of my childhood, gave me strength to deal with loneliness, and I thank him with all my heart.

WAGSY

The first time I remember getting depressed I'd probably wanted to do something and my mother hadn't sanctioned it. I was kicking stones around the neighborhood and up the alley at the house next door there was a little dog baring his teeth, yapping and snapping at me and I thought, here is someone who wants to talk to me. So I squatted down, trusting his chain to hold him, and very slowly let my hand move up towards his face with me talking, "Hi, Wagsy, good doggy. I know you like me." What a funny name for such a nasty little dog. When a dog is yapping viciously, it's not wise to go fast. So slowly my hand was reaching towards him. Then I could see his eye on my hand as he was yapping at me, and he was secretly sniffing it, barking and sniffing.

So gradually that it was almost imperceptible, I got to where my hand was in a place where he could decide whether to make a lunge, which wasn't going to work, or whether to give me a cheek I could scratch. And he decided the latter. He wanted a little girl to scratch his cheek. And so I did. I remember his eyes closing. It was a great occasion for both of us. He let me scratch his cheek. So I was petting him and he was at the far end of his chain. There was a fence there, it was something I could climb over, but I didn't on that day. We sat within reach and there was some possibility of the hand being bitten, still. Well, that dog was terribly important in his way, although I never could get him to stop biting everybody else but me and maybe his owners.

I have noticed that when I get just miserable, I relax, droop, slow down – a very slowing down thing happens to me. Being depressed is kind of a great thing. You can relax into it. It's good to go outside and then you want to look at something besides what you're depressed about. So you find yourself studying ants, or little creatures come up to you. Or maybe you even have the sense to grab some raw sunflower seeds when you go out the door and you can see if anybody wants to eat them if you keep really, really still.

I had to be depressed, or it wouldn't have happened. I would have just skipped on by. I mean a kid wouldn't go up to a yappy little dog unless she felt like she really wanted company. And there was nobody else in the world who wanted to talk to her.

Wagsy was not a good boy. He bit everybody. He bit anybody he could reach. But I made friends with him. I was five. When his owner saw me playing with him out in the back yard, she came running out saying, "You can't…!" Then she saw that he was lying on his back, wanting his belly scratched. She didn't know what to make of it.

It was maybe a year later my cousin Joan came over. Mom said, "You girls go out and play." She was a couple of years older and I didn't know how to entertain her. So, you know, the burden of responsibility. It was beyond me. Then I thought, well, maybe she'd like to do what I had done, learn to tame little Wagsy. I said, "Come on!" Poor girl. He barked and snarled at her. She just hated the thought of playing with him. She started to cry. I said, "Come on!" I went over to Wagsy and said, "Now be a good boy." But I couldn't make him stop snarling at her.

Overcoming an animal's fear was a big deal. It made me feel like I could do things with animals that other people couldn't, or wouldn't, because my cousin didn't even try.

Some time later, Wagsy got loose in the neighborhood. The lady next door came over and asked my mother, would your little girl get my dog? He got off his chain and he's terrorizing the neighborhood. I was seven then and was sent out to do this job. I was very proud. Looking around, I could see curtains pulled back with faces in windows. Up the street I could see a boy up in a tree. I saw Wagsy there under the boy in the tree and I walked up slowly. I got to him and he wagged his tail at me. He was very pleased to see me. He seemed to say, "Let's go together, you and I. I'll take care of you. I'll protect you from everything." Briefly, I considered his offer. But I knew that protection was the least of my needs. I needed my supper and I needed blankets to sleep in. I realized that if he sensed me refusing that, he wouldn't be catchable. So I bent over and picked him up. He was just a little guy. And I carried him and we talked and I scratched his cheek and behind his ear and he licked my hand and closed his eyes as we walked slowly down the sidewalk.

I felt like a magical hero. Everybody was watching, the kid in the tree and all the people behind the curtains as this little girl walked carrying this little dog in her arms down the street. I wanted to go as slow as possible because it was a precious moment. But also, I knew he was going to want to jump and run. I think what happened was that he had trusted me not to take him home. So when I arrived and his owner took him from me there was this moment of trying wildly to get away. I really felt bad about that. She grabbed him and got a good hold on him.

Not long after that she came over and asked my mother if her little girl would like to have Wagsy. My mother looked at me because I was right there. I thought, I can't handle him at all. So I had to say "No" because the neighbor woman said she could send him "out to the farm." If he lived on a farm, he could apply his energies to protecting animal feed from rats. Maybe there would be a little girl on the farm and they could run and play together. If he lived on a farm, he could be happy. I didn't know what "sending him to the farm" meant. It took years before I knew what it meant.

Notes

When I was thirty-one, I came to a time when I was depressed again and needed to connect with myself and I needed to write, but I couldn't imagine writing anything beyond a daily journal, and the same mood or zone that caused me to want to write also caused the small birds to come to my hand. And so, for something like a year or so, I wrote a journal of the birds who came to my hand.

BIRD JOURNAL

It's funny how things get started. One Christmas I received two bird feeders. And what's amazing I guess is how seldom I wonder what my life would have done with itself if they had given me pillowcases. I just dove in to what was here.

At first, I had one of the feeders hanging on the front porch but no birds ever came to it and finally a chipmunk came and gathered it all. He filled his cheek pouches and rushed off, then came back for more. After a couple of hours, towards the bottom of the little feeder, it was very funny and thrilling because he had to get in the thing. But then because of him I had to move it and I moved it to a tree about fifty feet away from the house that I could see through the big window. All that winter it was almost entirely Steller's jays and in the spring the chipmunks found it again and I discontinued it.

In the fall, I started again after the chipmunks had got themselves holed up, this time moving the plastic feeder to a tree branch outside the big window about five feet from the house and the box feeder in the back twenty feet from the window.

Things went along dully enough until one day the Pips came. I found out later that they're Nuthatches. Saucy, courageous mischievous little critters about the size of Chickadee with the soul of a wildcat. What got me really looking was one day soon after the Pips arrived, a lone fat-beaked junco type came to the box feeder and decided to settle down right there. I could see in the trees round about there piled up a dozen or so birds waiting in line fussing and fidgeting like people in line for the telephone booth or the bathroom. But Fat-beak wouldn't budge. He was about twice the size of Pip. Pip and Chickadee both tried to scare him off the feeder by swooping close but Fat-beak was determined to settle down there. Pip has this amazing ability to walk down a tree headfirst and he finally got the notion that did the job. He got a couple of feet above Fat-beak on the trunk of the tree and started down the tree circling the trunk. When he caught Fat-beak's eye about six inches away, he fanned out his tail, raised his wings, puffed himself up and slowly pivoted holding this pose. Fat-beak actually fell off the feeder in a dither and went to a distant tree. I saw him again the next day but after that he was gone.

A few weeks later something happened which somewhat colored my tender admiration of Pip (Pip is a pair, but I can't tell one from the other, so I call them both Pip). The box feeder has a little roof on hinges which can be flipped up to put in more seeds, and the jays have found it convenient to land on the roof in such a way as to open it and get at the seeds that way rather than properly from the bottom. One day the roof was up and there were few seeds and as I was absent-mindedly looking out the window, I saw Chickadee fly into the feeder so I could see him through the glass. He seemed to be having a nice little orgy in there with all those seeds, but then Pip started swooping again and again in quick succession and I rushed out and lifted the glass. Pip retreated in mid-swoop and Chickadee had presence of mind to carry a sunflower seed in his retreat. But I felt I had saved him from being badly tormented by Pip.

A month or two after the arrival of the Pips one morning I looked out and saw the Tigers. What a sight. Such elegant timorous birds, though their name is Canadian tree sparrow, they have rust-and-steel-gray markings on their heads, white bellies and tiger stripes on their backs. Also they have a black spot over their heart. I thought there was a pair like the Pips but a few days later, I saw the three of them, the third being periodically chased off and coming back. Weeks later, as I write, this still goes on.

Finally I decided that suet would be helpful so I went to the meat market and got a whole bunch of it, put a hunk of it on a nail I pounded into a little tree right by the big table. I was surprised to see that it was just fat. The first and biggest batch the dog got before anyone came so the second piece was smaller. And they came, they really came to it, right by the big table even. Chickadees came and Pip and Steller's jays and finally timid Tiger came. Also came a funny pair one day, unnamed, unrelated, one is a sort of a Pip, that is, he's shaped like Pip but I haven't seen him go down a tree, as a matter of fact I've seen him avoid that act. Also his feathers are mottled in a most

beautiful way looking very like winter fur, silver and
black with maybe a touch of auburn. Brown creeper, I believe. The other is a junco type, big and soft and downy,
soft gray on top and soft white on the bottom with a line
between gray and white which is parallel with the ground,
so he looks like he swam duck-fashion once in Clorox. He
has a yellow beak.

So the birds came to the suet and at night the dog
took away what was left so that in the morning I must
needs go out again with a new piece. And thus I an-
nounced myself to the birds as the center of their good
fortune or, as Neowyn put it, I am the Feeding Woman.
Actually, I am highly honored by their presence. When I
walk through the woods, I find birds scarce and I realize
that they are really gathered here. I don't understand why
the gray jays don't come. They flutter about the edges not
coming close enough to get anything. But they manage
somehow to be fat and fluffy so I shouldn't worry, but I
do because they are so beautiful and have such expres-
sions. My cousin tells me they swoop down and take a
bite of a sandwich in someone's hand. I did have a nice
conversation with one once in the big meadow. I was trying to mimic him and he was giving me lessons and I
came quite close but he didn't come down from his
branch.

Well, so somehow the gray jays don't come and I will look into that and the magpies don't come although I've seen them too on the edge wanting to come. A few days ago one was actually on the ground in the trees about a hundred feet away. I think he was pretending to be here, hopping about on the ground not finding anything. He must have known about the suet. He looked too big for the forest floor. He looks right on the topmost branches of tall trees.

We went along with the suet for a couple of weeks I guess, and it didn't take long for the news to get around. The size of the group must have tripled in those two weeks.

Then one sunny chilly day after I had forgotten the suet for a day or two, that day then I went out with a big hunk of suet in my hand and my big fur cape. I was dreamy and very sad, in an anguish of sorrow and want but dreamy, you understand, not screaming at all, too dreamy to scream. In any case I was walking slowly with this big hunk of suet and a chickadee swooped down fluttering like a leaf in autumn towards the suet but he chickened out twice. I was, as you can imagine, standing quite still by then, hoping he'd get the courage but I was still dreamy and the third time he did land on the suet, grabbed a bite and flew precipitately away to eat it.

My life since then has taken a very different course than it would have done otherwise. As I put the suet on the nail I had the thought that maybe the birds could give me reason to go on living awhile longer.

The next day I went out walking real slow and calling them. I guess I hadn't told you that. I had been calling them every time I went out to them - "Hey, Pip! Come Tiger, Chickadee?" So they'd be sure to know I was there. He came down then after only one swoop and he came to me right off the next time and took time for four bites before he left. And I went around after that telling everyone how the birds were coming to me and my mother called me Saint Francis and most everyone else looked blank, I don't know why. It was right about in here that a chickadee threw himself against the window and died. It was a very painful scene in every way. I rushed to the window and saw him lying on his back, his eyes closed and his beak opening and closing. It immediately occurred to me that he was having his last words. By the time I got out there, he was dead. I picked him up in my hand – such a little thing in my hand, though round and firm – I don't know how they can eat so much or how they can be so feisty and noisy and impressive. Bite-size. One bite. I took him to a place under a tree where there was no snow and the pine needles were deep. And I buried him there under the pine needles since the ground was too frozen to consider cutting into. As I walked with his corpse and from his grave, I could hear chickadees around me and I couldn't tell whether they were speaking of him or of me. I found myself worrying about my reputation among chickadees. I felt sure from the beginning that he wasn't one of those that I had noticed or the particular one that had come to me but I was greatly reassured when a chickadee came to a branch by where I was walking and looked at me and chattered in an amiable way, seeming to me to say that the good spirits of the Chickadees and my good reputation were okay somehow still. Perhaps the casualty was a newcomer.

One day I went out – it was warm out – I went and sat with the suet in my lap and the friendly chickadee came and took a bite of suet. He had to hop about on my legs to get to it, which felt wonderfully strange; a track that was more of a grip than a weight. He came back several times, five I think was the count, in about an hour and a half. It was quite an experience. For one thing, I felt very upset because I couldn't tell one chickadee from another, so every chickadee was a potential friendly one so that when he arrived it was always a shock. He first came to the ground ten feet or so away and hopped in zigzags toward me. This I found to be an often-repeated pattern. I feel that the main objective was to give me a chance to strike while he still had the chance to fly.

The next time I went out I sat for an hour on the wet ground in the cold breeze and nobody came and I was very sad. I thought they had left me. Or actually, I thought I must have been having the wrong vibrations. Somebody had spoken to me about vibrations when I said the birds were coming to me, that I must have changed my vibrations towards birds so I thought maybe I had changed them back again. And I was making a study of my vibrations and saw that perhaps while I was sitting there that time I was unsatisfiable so perhaps they figured why should they try.

The next time I went out I took suet and also sunflower seeds because I felt that since there was suet in three places it would be too demanding to expect them to come to that in my lap. So I had a little seashell with sunflower seeds in it on the ground by me as well as the suet in my lap. The friendly one came once to the suet then the horses came. Blueboy the Welsh pony made me laugh by persisting in eating my hair and licking my forehead. Finally after each horse had carefully inspected me – none found the sunflower seeds which I had hidden under my coat – they left me in peace.

I was watching Pip then in astonishment because I could see that now there were three Pips and two were males because they fanned out their tails. It was very tense. One male would chase the female gloriously around a tree then the other male would attack him breaking the arc of their glorious dance at an oblique angle. Then the two males would light on two separate trees about ten feet apart and in a great flurry and uproar they would hop about having positions at each other. Finally one fanned his tail and raised his wings as I described before (when Fat-beak was hogging the feeder months before) and when he did that, the other flew off. This was all accomplished in about three seconds or maybe five but then it was repeated variously over and over. They also fought over the feeder.

But at the same time that all that was going on, I was distracted by the arrival of the jays. It was two gray jays and three Steller's jays. What a day. The Steller's jays were watching the gray jays, keeping in relation to them, that is they would fly a second after the gray jays would fly and in a parallel direction. The gray jays were definitely looking me over. They were in a formation always, which really impressed me. He was watching me and she was always watching him, or was it the other way around? But it seemed to be quite complex. She seemed to be covering for him. At first they were behind me, he ten yards from me and scratching, which seemed important; I presume it holds the same importance for him as it does for Marlon Brando.

She was further on in the trees and more obscure; he was definitely looking me over. Now as I think of it, it must have been the one I call "she" who came into my tree. What happened was there was a sudden whir and I feared that everyone was startled and going away. But what did happen was that all the jays moved from one place to the other and for a couple of seconds it was an astonishing sight like Grand Central Station: jays were very busy and going somewhere all over the place. So I didn't see which gray jay it was who did land in my tree and which it was who was five yards off to my left and scratching. I had presumed that it was he who was nearest who came quite near but in fact when I think of the scratching, it must have been she who came to my tree and looked down at me. It was really funny to see her struggles to do this. She had to get a hold on a twig sideways so that she was kind of sticking out then turn her head till her eye was actually aimed, then straight down at me. I was leaning against the trunk. It would perhaps have been more sensible to stand up comfortably in a nearby tree like he was there scratching but I did appreciate the effort and the closeness.

I must have done the wrong thing somehow or perhaps expected too much. I wanted them to come to the suet and I expected them to find me okay and come down. Actually I may have had the wrong vibrations again because I thought when they do come, I'll just faint because they are so beautiful and have such eyes and I may have thus been putting out too much to them. Finally they left then, seemingly in boredom, certainly in a great whir and flurry. Just after that, I was looking intently at something I don't remember what and I heard a small rustle at the sunflower seeds at my side and knew that the friendly chickadee was at them. He came back five times in quick succession before I deigned to look at him and then he came back a dozen or so more times to the shell. Then came once almost to my feet a timorous little chickadee with a mottled mask and I had hopes and said, "well howdy, Freckles" but he flew off and I was cold then and went in.

A week or two after that there came a downy woodpecker and the whole swarm of rosy finches and now I have to fill the feeders twice as often and the yard is constantly atwitter. Every time the donkey snorts or anybody scratches his head or swats at a fly or yawns or moves a foot, fifteen or twenty rosy finches fly off screaming and it sounds like they're saying, "The sky is falling, the sky is falling!" But usually one or two are still there on the ground unconcernedly eating. I don't see how they can do that unless they're blind and deaf which they're not or else they're sophisticated and actually think some decadent thing like "Mob rule is bunk." These rosy finches are really very strange and interesting. There are four different color patterns within a general pattern. The individuals seem to be as differentiable as any domestic animal and so the immediate conclusion is of course that they have their own domesticity, that is, a social organism that works well enough that an individualist or a rebel can survive.

One day I found that my suet was going moldy so I dumped it by the front porch then like a fool I took an unmoldy piece and went to my usual place under the tree in the back. After about ten minutes I had the distinct feeling that I wasn't "where it's at" like they say, and disconsolately I started back in the house and there was Stan sitting on the front porch exclaiming about how I had tamed the birds because they were coming in great quantities and pecking at that suet right at his boot. And so we sat together on the porch and the chickadees came and busily dispatched the moldy suet. I hope it didn't disagree with

them. I see it didn't kill them anyway. There must have
been twenty chickadees coming and going in that suet.
No other species came while we were there, although the
juncos hovered around but didn't brave that nearness. So
I guess in fact the word has gone around among the
chickadees that we are as it says on the sunflower seed
package "Birds' Best Friend." But interspecies communication is perhaps slow and so far it's only the chickadees
who feel well enough assured although I see that some of
the others are watching me closely.

Last week I sat under the tree as before and waited
but nobody came in the hour that I sat there. But there
was an excitement. It was Red. I had seen him the day before arrive with his two wives. He's a lovely little sparrow
type with a crimson blotch on his head, which fades to
pink on his belly and out to nothing on his rump and tail.
Under the crimson are the usual sparrow or finch lines of
gray-brown along each feather and a white background
and a paler belly. His wives were this way but with no
crimson. I hear he's a house finch.

Anyway, he started singing while I was sitting there
and his gestures were swinging his head back and forth
like a canary when he's really going. Well, Red really got
going in that tree and went through a whole spiel. Then
he went to another tree and looked around for a couple of

minutes and then went through the spiel again. It was really lovely. I felt that it was definitely a song of possession. A formal bow, a discreet glance to be sure he wouldn't be stepping on anyone's toes, a careful delicate warming-up period then the proclamation, long-winded and elegantly done and within the proper form. I heard an introduction and several repetitive verses, covering perhaps the branch, the tree, and the four directions, also the sky above and the ground beneath; the sort of thing that went out with the nineteenth century or maybe earlier. I was also astonished at his energy and endurance as he was at it at top pitch almost the whole time I was there. I also felt that I was an important part of his audience.

I have, by the way, noticed that it's no easy kick being a bird. The effort, the alertness, the coordination, the constant excitement are at all times evident. I haven't yet seen a little bird in any attitude that I'd call restful. The sunflower seeds they have to hammer violently with their whole bodies swinging behind the beak for maybe fifteen seconds for each one. And flying takes so much tension and constant calculation and caution and balance. Well. Free as a Bird, indeed. They're hard workers.

Today as I was hanging out clothes there came to a nearby tree a Steller's jay who then proceeded to sing. His song was soft and exceedingly dissonant. He popped about in a great range seeming to enjoy going further than an octave in speed and control. The sound comes out very like some of John Cage's music and I have named him John Cage. I think the Steller's jays have a thing where they mimic the sounds they hear. There's one that makes like our neighbor's vent.

Now I have sat out under the tree again with an enormous hunk of suet on my lap and I am filled with despair because I was treated like a human being and because I haven't seen the friendly chickadee since Stan and I were sitting on the porch and he came and Stan said what is his name? And I said Feisty and he said Rusty? And I said Feisty and then Feisty flew off. That was over a week ago now and I am very worried and upset and yesterday as I say I was treated with utmost suspicion. There were two notable things that happened though. One was the manner of a pair of jays. They were lovers in the old tradition. He went to the feeder and got some seeds then flew to her right up beside her and jammed the seeds into her mouth. Then he went again to the feeder and got some seeds and she waited and fidgeted but he was just eating and she flew to another branch and posed. I don't know how it came out though because I was distracted by the other thing which was a very lovely male gray squirrel who ran busily from tree to tree, the first I've seen this year though

I've heard them for a couple of weeks. I was interested to see that he went into the outhouse, which is a favorite haunt for them or perhaps he's the only one. There are enormous heaps of pinecone fragments from last year proclaiming a particular bag of cloth to be a favorite spot to sit upon and eat undisturbed. I got some seeds in my hand and offered them to him and he became both enticed and angry and he was very funny about it. He ran from tree to tree desiring and scolding and I named him Bildad. But he finally talked himself into caution and the jays were gone and I was suddenly sad and went in.

Just this morning I was coming out with a bag of suet for the tree that's further out to feed the shy ones and I stopped on the porch because there was a chickadee at the suet on the porch and I didn't want to disturb him so I was standing there with my bag of suet and somehow there were six or eight chickadees then playing games around that suet on the porch. And I guess just like anybody else, one damn fool chickadee went swooping gaily around and he swooped right into the handle of the wheelbarrow with a crash. It was pretty terrible. There he was then sitting on his belly instead of his feet and his beak was open and his eyes were half shut and he was kind of swaying. I was sitting then leaning into him, not knowing whether I should pick him up or bury him or what. I went over and sat in the mud and looked closely at him. Once I tried to pick him up but he fluttered "No" so I sat beside him and looked while he swayed. I tried again to pick him up and this time he climbed up into my hand though I don't credit him with trust but only with being half-unconscious and not finding me too objectionable. So I picked him up and he was so light that I really could hardly feel him and his mouth was open and his eyes half shut and he was leaning against the heel of my hand. I expected him to die in my hand but he didn't. Gradually I saw his eyes become more open and at the same time felt his feet grip my hand and he stood or actually squatted in my hand and he was looking about rather dully and I began to think he might live though his mouth was still open. Then I wondered if he had a broken jaw and if so what would I feed him and all the time I felt like I was being watched by thirty or forty eyes. He got up then and went to my finger, which was the top of my hand and I felt that it was beginning to fog in on him where he was. Then he went to my knee, the obvious taking-off place and then he closed his beak, for which I would have liked to cheer but I refrained from cheering. He stood then on my knee and looked around, seeming to be getting his bearings and he did look at me a few times and he took his time, for which I was grateful, though I knew already that he was not in my hand anymore and I was sorry. But in my honor I must say I was more glad to see him fine than sorry he wasn't mine. I remember Blake was clear about that once.

> "He who binds to himself a joy,
> Doth the winged life destroy.
> He who kisses the joy as it flies,
> Lives in Eternity's sunrise."

So of this episode there is little more to tell. Finally as soon as he looked as though he could, he flew off, straight and true. I sat then in my chair feeling very nice and a bit dazed and the chickadees came back in swarms and I got out the sunflower seeds and etc.

Some days later as I was out shoveling donkey-shit to make a compost heap, I saw that it seemed that the birds were actually attuning themselves to me in hopes of having some sort of party. I have sort of wondered about this before. Anyway, as I walked past a suet tree, I heard the Oregon chickadee holler. Where the others have white eyebrows, his head is just solid black and also his voice is loud and rasping. So he hollered and there were his wife and him and also Pip and his wife. I think I mentioned about the three Pips. Well, now there only seem to be two but as I can't tell them apart, I don't know how it came out or where the third one went. Well, there were these four birds in the suet tree hopping about and slowly, very slowly, I approached until I was three feet from the suet and I swear they were putting on a show for me or having a party with me of some sort. They fought over branches nearest to me and they acted very excited. Finally I was only a foot away from the suet and Oregon and Pip had chickened out mostly, only making quick attempts at courage but failing while Feisty and three of his kin were all there and whirring around my head and looking into my eyes. It seemed to be some very complex musical chairs scene that I couldn't altogether figure out. My main problem was the terribly shameful difficulty of not being able to tell them apart. I suppose the most civilized thing to do would be tag them in some way but it seems to me that something crucial would be lost thereby, I'm not sure just what it is, but it may be the basic object of this study, if such it may be called.

Then I was out raking in the front and I saw in the big window a junco making the most beautiful gestures trying to get out of the house. He looked like the greatest dream of the ballet, though at the time I didn't appreciate his beauty but ran up the hill shouting "NO! NO! NO!" but now as I remember his movements and know it came out all right, I find him to be so beautiful. I do believe that it was he that ballet was inspired by in the first place. His fluttering was like Maria Tallchief or the ballerina in "Red Shoes." I was quickly there and then what to do? With my hand and my presence I kind of aimed him hopefully toward the door but I could see that from that angle, there was no sky out the door and so he didn't go there; he went to the other window and danced like when she's had the red shoes on for a long time and she's fagging out with despair. I was worried and my hands were shaking which was too bad; I may have got more trust from him had they not been. So he fluttered about and I fluttered about. Finally he did trust me, that is he gave up the saving of his life by the usual channels and he stood there on the windowsill long enough for me to surround him with my trembling hands. He had a second thought then and tried with an astonishing amount of strength to get out of my hands but I didn't let him. Quickly I took him out the door and opened my hands and he scudded hastily away.

Yesterday I went out to feed them and Pip came up to me and it was strange. He makes these wonderful little noises like a confident puppy. And he made it and came quickly to me. I think he was saying, "Wait! Wait!" so I waited and he came so close to my face I must have been cross-eyed looking at him. I believe I saw the strain in his face as he looked over his shoulder at me, which is a peculiar gesture they all seem to have. If they're afraid, they turn their backs and peer over their shoulders. I guess the threat is that they'll fly off if you make a false move.

I have one more thing to tell before going. It's April 13, Thursday, and we're going for three weeks, which is too bad because I'll miss the spring and all the new birds coming one by one.

But it's absolutely necessary that I go so it must be that it will be all right. Well, it's snowing and everybody's fussed and the rosy finches are here in groups of thirty or forty and eating the seeds on the windowsills. I'd always noticed that one or another was constantly jumping up but now I'm seeing I think the beginning of the mating season in the rosy finches. Two face each other puffed up and beaks in air then facing each other they rise fluttering straight into the air with beaks and bellies almost touch-ing. I think the deal is to fly higher. Anyway, it's decisive. When they come down, one goes away and the other gets the prize. At this time, the prize seems to be seeds. A little bit ago, I saw four face each other in a circle but they couldn't get it off the ground.

Well, tomorrow I go to fly in airplanes and perhaps I will feed pigeons in New York City before the next story.

Hello! I'm back! I've been back over a week and we had a wonderful time and I'm glad to be back but have forgotten how to write. I've been doing a lot of gardening and the birds have come close to me. The first two days I went hollering around the house proclaiming my return in case nobody noticed and one time Chickadee swirled round my head like a fly as I was standing on the porch then landed on a beam near me and I said "Chickadee!" and he flew away. I wish I understood that. (Years later I discovered that "Chickadee!" is their territorial call & chases them away.) While we were gone, the babysitters said that two magpies came to the suet and then also have arrived loud and numerous the red-winged blackbirds. One hummingbird came to the hummingbird feeder two days before we came back but he hasn't returned.

Red the house finch and his two wives both of whom I call Maw are here. They have a strange personality. Again with shame I find I can't tell them apart. They are both stolid and fearless, able to eat off the windowsill and look at me through the glass. Sometimes I've seen one sit on the feeder and eat for half an hour or more with other birds flitting about, even eating with her.

I think I'm not doing very well really, although some nice things have happened. Perhaps it's because of every-body having babies now. I guess I'll think of it that way. But I don't feel the remotest possibility that someone might come to my hand. I sat yesterday morning with a big hunk of suet in my lap and the woods were quiet. Then I became worried because once a Steller's jay flopped away behind me and I jumped and so I think I am in some vibration trouble because I should not have jumped. Maybe a rest would help. No. We'll see about that.

I've been doing a lot of gardening, especially by one suet-bag where, while I've been gardening, have come two chickadees. They are a sweet pair who are always together and who allow me to be a foot away and the Pips are also very close and a hairy and a downy woodpecker. Hairy was maybe ten feet away; the Downy is looking at me as I write, five feet away. They are really grand the way they do everything with their necks.

A pair of broad-tailed hummingbirds has come now all day to their feeder right outside the window above the kitchen sink. What grace! What elegance! Such grand colors! But mainly I find something incredibly haunting about the hummingbird's carriage.

Yesterday I sat on the porch and listened to the hummingbirds' sound, which seems to be made with their wings. After I had sat a while, a chipmunk came and ate the seeds at my feet and two other chipmunks were watching him to see if he would live through that. One was his mate and the other was not really a chipmunk, maybe twice his size and with patches on his sides of white and black. A golden-mantled ground squirrel. The chipmunks which are smaller than a robin and bigger than a junco have many stripes and live as they also did last year in the rocks of the terrace under the sculpture only last year they never came near me. So anyway that was pleasant only even the juncos didn't dare join us. But today it started raining and then it snowed so the juncos came to the seeds on the windowsills and there were lots and lots of them and also there was a new bird I don't know who but it has the same fighting scene as the juncos. There were two of them alike with white helmets. They were bigger than the juncos and they did sort of join them and keep an eye on them not out of any fear – quite the contrary – but for tips as to what to do and how to act and even, and I was astonished, they were up on the windowsills right away. Their tails, of uniform brownish tan color, did fan out when they were snapping at each other and once I went out and one of them went hoppity-hop down the road like in the kids' primer.

I want to say something about the red-winged blackbirds. For one thing, I've finally seen a female or two, drab they are and smaller and shy and timorous. But they have the same funny gawky gestures of pecking with their shoulders and flipping their tails. I'm pretty sure they flip their tails like that in case someone comes up behind them, it might scare that person away. They don't always do it but just when they feel a little paranoid. Then there is the funny way that the males handle the red on their shoulders: on the bottom of the red is a yellow strip. When they feel bucolic, they take and cover absolutely all the red with black feathers and even into the yellow; but if anyone threatens them they display the red broadly and of course when they fly. It's like two scarlet blobs in a black container.

The hummingbirds are coming now to their feeder constantly and it is possible at the kitchen sink to get within a foot or two of them. They are forever humming and swooping about.

They shoot over the trees from distant places as though they were shot from guns. Then they stop at the feeder and the humming changes as they sip. If they feel secure, they just keep their bills in the stuff for maybe a minute, their miniscule white tongue evidently a tube through which they suck. But as their bills stand still at

the honey-water, their wings are going – it said in a book
fifty-five times in a second – and so that's a blur with
some suggestion of the shape of feathers in the bottom-
most position. The funny part is the way their asses waggle then as they keep their heads still. I guess something
has to waggle with the wings but you know one never
thinks of it that way.

A couple of days ago coming home from a walk we
must have flushed some juncos off the porch as we came
up and there was one woozy junco in the dirt who must
have banged into a barrel that's there and I picked him up
although my hands were cold and it was a bad time of day
with kids swarming around and shouting. But I sat in the
rocking chair and my hands became immediately warm
but not sweaty and I warmed this little bird in my hands
and I felt sure he would live because he didn't look as bad
as that chickadee I had sat with some weeks ago. Then I
moved my hand a little and he angrily fluttered out of my
hands onto my knee and he glared at me from my knee
and shat on it. Then sadly enough the school bus came
and he fluttered rather clumsily up onto the porch beam.
Then when I opened the door for the kids he flew away
and half an hour later he was on the windowsill and I rec-
ognized him.

On that walk we flushed a pair of ducks and we found I'm sure they were nests all soggy on the ground. I thought they had come down in last week's hail. I worry about things like that although I know it is madness to do so. I think I do it because I so much want to be there when some such personal catastrophe happens and (I have a long romance on the subject in my head) then I might honorably take home a bird that for a while might be dependent on me and I might develop a relationship not based on thirty-second encounters. Funny thing, and somehow perhaps proof that the whole thing is imaginary is that there is a canary in a cage in this house and all he seems to do in my studies is goad me on to the wild birds who seem more available.

It's been six weeks or so since I've spoken to you though I've thought of lines to put in like "This morning I awoke and looked out the window and there were a hum-mingbird sipping sugar-water and a woodpecker eating suet on our front porch." But then I couldn't go on. This morning again there was a hummingbird and a wood-pecker only this time we two humans also sitting on the porch. Then of course there are dozens of Steller's jays and juncos. I must tell you that the juncos have separated now. There are never more than two or three together. It's almost as if they've been mostly slaughtered but I know it's just their habit to arrive *en masse* in the spring and then separate in the summer. The chickadees come still to the suet. I see one that I don't know and who is shy with me. Pip is here too. His manner delights me. And the red-winged blackbirds and everyone come to the windowsills where I put a couple quarts of seeds a day which are mostly eaten by the chipmunks and ground squirrels which I told you about. But everyone comes to the windowsills: juncos, jays, Pip, redwings. But not the chickadees and not the woodpeckers. They don't come to the feeders either. I guess since they both come to the suet on the porch that it can't be shyness. More likely better stuff is easily available in the trees around.

The hummingbirds are astonishing. Every evening – we have very long evenings, excruciating – they come for a last good sip to last the night. Four or five at a time they come, but not at all are they together. They have the geometric squabble scene that I described with the juncos only with some geometrical differences. First that the object to get to is a single point, the feeder, and second that they have three dimensions to fight in. Only the males come in the evening, it being too much geometry for the females to bear. Though there is one female who has been coming in the evenings, the same one every time, but she seems some sort of an "in-between", with a big ruby blotch on her neck. There are two other females with a few ruby feathers on their necks but she takes the cake. The females, being speckled as they are, can be easily told apart; there seems lots of room for variations in the speckles. That is, there is the in-between, and there's the one with two ruby specks, and then there's Three Black Dots, and the Little Pale One and Brown Spots and Three Ruby Spots. There are two or three more too, which means, figuring an equal number of males, well over a dozen hummingbirds living here with us. I wouldn't be surprised if it was two dozen. And they finish off a feeder-ful in a little less than a day, which fact had me constantly on the alert to fill it until finally I went and bought an-other one. In the evening I went out to the established feeder thinking to join in the evening's fun and at the same time introduce the new feeder. So I went with it full. It has a wire they can perch on unlike the old one where they have to buzz their wings while drinking. Anyway, I went with a couple of kids watching and I arrived in the midst of the geometry, which wasn't affected by my pres-ence much, except perhaps to change the shape in the ge-

ometry. I held up the new feeder and after some confusion and hesitation, one male came and perched and
sipped slowly then was chased away. But the chaser hadn't
the nerve to come to the new feeder and got chased himself from the old one, by one who only dared to take a
tiny sip before being chased away by yet another who just
flew away himself from nerves I guess, and there was a
moment of silence and then it all happened over again.
The "in-between" came and drank from the new feeder
still in my hand. I have noticed that the females are more
brave or, as one young man put it, the males are more
cautious. The males have a lovely masculine gesture that
they do with their tails and I've not seen the females do it
at all, even the in-between. Usually, their tails are small
and insignificant, but when they chase off another hummingbird, they bend it in a very horny and lovely way and
it's dark red though not luminous like the throat.

I was going to tell you about a fly. Although I know it's not a bird and all that, it seemed to me to be very important. A few days ago we acquired three chameleons in a clear plastic box with sand and a cactus and we feed them mealworms which are a penny apiece, and also Stan catches flies alive for them and puts them in the box and they like flies better than mealworms. Now when I look at the chameleons I can see that they are the image of the dragons in the movies. They are really terrible. Their mouths are a big smile of a flapping trap and their heads are flat and their eyes roll and click shut and open. And when they're upset, up sprouts a stiff ridge along the backbone and the dewlap under the lower jaw can suddenly expand into a red ax-shape and they then proceed to chop up and down jerkily with their whole bodies as the ax handle.

Well, so, they are impressive-looking fellows and to-day Stan put a perfectly healthy-looking buzzing fly into the box and it walked up to one of these monstrous-looking dragons and just keeled over dead.

There is one more image on which I think to end this volume of my journal. It was at the very first when I had not yet received the feeders and I was hanging up clothes and it was spring. Above me was a great whirring and a hundred rosy finches came down and landed all around me in the trees and on the roof and the ground around. Happily I had been feeding the horses oats, so there was something for them to peck at, and as I continued to hang up clothes very slowly, they strutted about burbling and twittering much like pigeons but they had just arrived and they were very excited and of course I felt honored and watched them with great excitement. They stayed around for maybe ten minutes then they all rose together and vanished beyond the trees.

Writing this gave me some courage at least that what I wrote might be readable and say something of interest, but it wasn't until nine years later that I realized I could write a story. A story is a very different thing. It has a beginning, a middle, and an end. And a punch line. It's an interesting form to work with, and I used it with delight for many years, trying each time to make some kind of a golden globe out of whatever happened. But in those nine years before I started writing stories, I wrote occasionally in my journal, and those pieces that had to do with animals I include here, scattered among the earlier pieces from the Lump Gulch period. Animals don't talk much in languages; but they totally do expect to be understood. They have a lot of respect for our intelligence and simply can't believe that we don't understand them. It's so obvious!

When I was a baby, the little pointy-eared dog named Points had taught me to recognize that she was somebody and I could understand her and obey her. This made it possible for me to see in Wagsy's snapping and snarling a cry of bitter loneliness. When I moved with my husband and children to Lump Gulch, it was possible for me to surround myself with all sorts of animals, and I conversed with them, one-to-one, all of them, reading their postures and moves and sounds as clearly as I could, with respect, predator and prey, both.

These animals of Lump Gulch taught me more and more across the years. There were goats and donkeys, chickens, ducks, geese, rabbits, a guinea fowl, a guinea pig, a snake and her food, mice. There were also, as I say, the wild animals, prey and predator. It seemed more than anything else that I needed to understand the animals. Because nobody else seemed to. And so, here are my stories mostly from Lump Gulch, though some are from different places, different times. Some are from when I was over eighty.

I begin with Tree, my closest friend in all my life. The first story I wrote about her, at her death, "Tree's Last Gift," can be found in <u>The Lady Orangutan and Other Stories</u>.

TREE

Tree had to have her horn amputated the other day. That was some scene, ten years old and goats don't live as long as dogs. Monday, lovely morning, I got up early and brought Sammy up to the greenhouse; she's (I hope she's a she, we don't have any place for a rooster) got a thing now about the oxalis flowers, eats them like they were fighting back, so I sat up there with her for quite awhile; how was I to know what had happened to Tree?

I always feel, once the goats are in Ida (that's the old car we use for a goat shed), that they're safe so I don't worry, but when I finally put Sammy in her box and got the milk bucket and the grain and went out there, I looked in Ida, and there was Tree with blood all over her face, all over the steering wheel, all over in the trunk. It was that horn that Rose had chewed a bite out of last year; I knew that was a bad thing when it happened, but then nothing actually came of it in all this time, so I didn't worry about it after awhile, but – whammo – there Monday morning was all that blood.

Well, it wasn't bleeding at the moment, so I opened the door, gave Daffy a cracker and left her in, just like every day and Tree ran to her stanchion, big full udder swinging back and forth as she ran and I locked her head in and milked her hard and fast; can't just leave her in the stanchion forever. Anyway, she can wiggle herself out in a couple minutes when she's done eating and sets her mind to it, so that's why I milked her fast and ran with the milk when she was only half done eating and I got the medicine off the shelf, picked up an old sock on the way, sopping it full of water, and ran out there.

She was just finishing up as I took the medicine and doused her horn good and washed her face with the wet sock; she wasn't too bad. She was pretty nervous and flippy, but she hadn't lost so much blood that she was out of her mind or anything, flippy but not floppy, and she depends on me. I've always done for her. I raised her in my lap with a bottle for starts, so she's like a daughter which is strange because now she's ten and an old lady while I'm only ten years older. Anyway, we're real close so it wasn't just any goat. In fact, no goat is just any goat. Every body is somebody. Even bugs.

As I went around Monday morning doing the laundry, I thought about it and I thought it might bleed like crazy again and the only thing to do was get that horn off that very day or else sleep with her in Ida which didn't sound too attractive, so I got on the phone and every goat person around was gone except old Mr. Umbarger who stutters but he knows a lot, he's had goats for years and he said I should have the vet de-horn her. "Th-th-th-them horns are no use to anybody, might as well t-t-t-t-take 'em both off at the base, but you better have the vet do it cause they b-b-b-bleed like anything. You wouldn't want to lose a good g-g-goat."

I didn't argue with him about it but it seems to me the horns on a goat are the handiest things for taking care of goats. You can take a goat wherever she doesn't want to go with 'em, stick her head in the stanchion, haul her into the car, all kinds of things.

There was only one local vet too at the moment, and nobody I knew could say anything about him so I called him cold and we got into it right away about taking 'em both off. "We might as well de-horn her entirely. Horns on a goat are a danger to the other goats and to their han-dlers as well. We'll just remove both horns down to the cranium."

I paused a moment, plowing past the nasty retorts. He was the last hope for a sanitary job done on the damn thing, so I hesitated and I said, "We use 'em for handle-bars," and we resolved to meet at five.

I put Daffy in Ida with half a flake of hay and used the other half to put Tree in Homer (that's the car I use for a vehicle) and we were off. Tree always rides in the front seat with her head on my shoulder, so there we were, and the first thing she did was whang her horn around on the back of the car seat and set to bleeding again. Jumpy as a cat she was at first, but then for the last twenty miles or so, she lay there, quietly dripping blood down my shirt. It wasn't as bad as before, and anyway, what could I do; I went on driving, trying to avoid bumps. Got there a few minutes early and the vet was a few minutes late, so we sat, slowly oozing. Tree was not feeling her best; she was bloated some and wouldn't chew her cud. She sat beside me and sighed while I fidgeted, hot sun beating down, no breeze, cement all around and blank walls, and nothing to say to each other. She knew why we were there.

I figured we'd have it out about de-horning, but when he arrived, he was okay. "Front seat privileges!" was what he said, and I knew he finally got the idea that Tree wasn't just an old goat, and then he said, "I've been thinking about it and I see no problem in taking off as little horn as is feasible," and then we were working together. I really like that, working together; it's a duet, two minds bouncing off each other toward the same goal. It brings the angels in every time. First he shaved around Tree's horn and

48

he could see right off how useful the horns were as I held her head steady as a rock, tipped it down a little so the hair wouldn't fall into her eye and in the shaved area he needled in a lot of Novocaine in little bits all around the horn, telling me how he doesn't like to cause pain.

That was the only time Tree was anything but perfectly well-behaved. She did try to climb up on me then but I held her firm and then he was done with that and she stood leaning her head into my knees as the stuff went to work and he got his equipment together. I was startled when he brought out his saw, looked like a miter saw and he washed it and dried it and sprayed it with disinfectant and came towards us with it in his hand.

Well, I said to myself, that's what we're here for, better accept it, so that's what I did. I backed up against Homer and held both Tree's horns, the bad horn below where he was to cut, there was still room for a good solid handgrip. I was the vise and he the carpenter, like when I was a kid and my dad made kitchen cabinets and I'd hold the board. But then the horn began to bleed as I knew it would and the vet hesitated and looked at the blood dripping down his mitre saw and then looked at me and I know my face was grim but I didn't flinch, I held on and waited so he went on with it, only faster.

That was a good sharp saw. Didn't take very long and the end of the horn was off and he ran with it to his truck and I looked at the end of the horn and it was replaced with a thin spray of blood almost a yard long coming out of white bone. It was like holding the garden hose but I knew I shouldn't put my thumb on it and when he ran back, I told him that and he agreed wholeheartedly as he got some powder and a piece of gauze and in careful haste slapped the powder on and whacked the gauze over it and it turned red as I pressed it on the smooth, flat stub, but it didn't drip much; then came the real bandage, looking very much like a sore thumb.

We rode back with her head in my lap.

ز&

I raised her in my lap with a bottle eighteen years ago, when I was thirty. Now I'm forty-eight and she's had a full life span.

I first got her and her sister when they were a month old, and a few days later they got into the birdseed and her sister died of bloat. Goats are so involved with each other, I feared that Tree would die of grief. I could see in her expression even then how she could imagine no happiness with her sister gone. That evening, I put her in the chair by my bed, pulled her attention to me. "Give me a chance," I said. And she did.

After that, she was devoted to me and I to her. We understood each other. We could reach each other's feelings. We'd take long walks, go places together, she'd show me things, follow me when I rode Rosco the donkey, ride in the car with her head in my lap. When her horns got long, I made her put her head on my shoulder. She wanted a goat, I gave her one. She couldn't stand to be without goats. I kept her in goats all her life. She had babies and loved them tenderly. She was a good milker, too; got me started making cheese.

One day, a dog attacked them and Tree got a bad bite on her back. All the other abrasions healed up but that one abscessed and I finally had to take her to the veterinarians in Ft. Collins. We arrived just as the vets were going out to lunch, and I could see they needed a break, so they took her into the stables. Presumably, they hadn't had much experience with goats, because she came running out a minute later, bleating. She looked like a wild creature, un-catchable, and I'm sure she would have been if they had chased her. But I bleated back as she had taught me to do, and she ran up to me and I waved my arm toward the inside of the car. She jumped in with what looked like utmost obedience, but it was to her a safe place, a place where she'd be under my care. I told the vets I had a sack lunch I could eat and Tree and I would wait for them in the car.

When they came back, we all went into a big dirt-floored building, and I stood holding her neck between my legs as a stanchion and she and I stood perfectly still for a long time while those two vets filled the area with local anesthetic and cut and cleared and washed and medicated that sore. The vets were amazed at her stillness for such a long time. "Oh," I explained, "She's smart. She knew what you were doing and she knew it'd be a big job. She just needed me to be involved."

She and the other goat, Fawn, wandered around the neighborhood for a couple of years until one neighbor decided to plant tulips, and of course, the goats ate the tulips so I had to build a fence. It had to be six feet high, so I asked our friend Charlie to build a palisade divided into two sections, one for the animals, an L-shape around the garden and the hay shed. It wasn't near as beautiful as goats grazing in the neighborhood, but it wasn't ugly, either. It had character. And it was plenty big. It provided a place where other animals could join the goats. I now had a barnyard.

I built the whole barnyard around her. Jack the donkey, chickens, geese, ducks. The high fence kept the dogs out. She was always queen of the yard. She became nasty with people, though. I had to quit taking her on walks with people. She'd rub up against them like a cat, then gradually up the ante, and pretty soon jab them in the crotch with a horn.

Not quite daily, but as often as I could, I would take the goats on a walk. We'd get past the houses pretty quick and go up the mountain a ways. Goats, dogs, donkey, we'd all go through the woods, up old wagon roads from the mining days. The goats and the donkey would want to graze in meadows and aspen groves.

Tree and I had a lifetime together, a goat's lifetime. New goats came into the barnyard, and Tree didn't have to tell them she was in charge. They just knew. Geese and ducks and chickens variously laid a lot of eggs. Tree liked to lean on Jack, the Donkey. I made lots of cheese from the goats, became known for my cheese. We didn't buy milk or cheese or eggs at the store, but probably paid more at the feed store and buying bales of hay. But the children enjoyed their fresh food from goats, chickens, and the garden. And I enjoyed having animals to commune with.

Walking through the woods and up and over the hills around us was nearly a daily event. Our place was a remnant of a ghost town. The cabin was originally built in 1890, along with several others. It was on a bit of a ridge that went west up to Old Baldy. To the south, across the road and across the creek was a lacework of wagon roads, remnants of the gold mining days. Tree and I and whoever came with us trailed through on those passageways, more just a wide place in the trees than anything. We'd stop and graze at the magic circle, a little spot, a circular open place, where across the years, as Tree and her friends grazed, I would marvel at its changes. When first I came to it, before I got Tree, the pond was deep enough that I could swim in it. But the next year was a dry year and somehow after that, it was never again deep enough to swim in. The frogs took over the pond, but the trees didn't move in. The circle remained open, as did the wagon roads, seemingly by tradition alone. We called it magic because it was a rare thing in those woods to find a space, about an acre or so, of sunshine and water. Mainly we called it magic because it made us happy. When the children came with us, they would wade and splash in it with great delight, a rare treat in the Rocky Mountains.

Tree and I roamed around the gulch together, finding places of interest, returning to check them out at another season. We'd go where we hadn't been before and we'd find things. Strawberry patches, havens to sit and rest in, beautiful rocks, amazing trees or groups of trees. Down by Ellsworth Creek we found a nameless grave. At the top of one of the wagon roads was a derelict cabin, the logs stuffed with 1896 newspapers, the walls papered with them. Bedsprings all over the place. Another cabin, room for a bed and a tiny stove, was built at the entrance to a mine hole called The Alice Mine, with narrow rail tracks running through the cabin to dump the ore on the mine dump. A convenient place to live and work. Remnants of the gold mining days a century ago were everywhere.

Tree and I led the others, whatever goats, dogs, donkey, humans. I knew she liked aspen groves and open spaces because it was good browsing; aspen groves, especially. She taught Fawn how to bend over an aspen sapling so that she could eat the leaves and then she would bend over another sapling for Fawn to imbibe. The little trees survived it and when they got bigger, they couldn't be bent. There were views I liked to go to, to study the clouds coming over the Continental Divide and see what weather was on its way.

The great thing with goats, and I'd imagine with all the ungulates, is proximity. Chewing their cuds together was a very nice, even an essential, thing to do. Siesta time

under the shade of a tree with a view in all directions
meant that everyone was a sentinel and all was peaceful.
Sitting amongst them in such a siesta was blissfully sooth-
ing. I'd have my lunch then, some sunflower seeds, perhaps an apple, water. Then after a while, we'd all rise up
and mosey back home.

One time, I saw Tree eating a mushroom, a very dangerous one, Amanita muscaria, very beautiful, actually,
orange with white spots. But I ran over and trampled the
rest of the mushroom into the ground and watched her to
see her reaction. The first sign was that she was not in
charge of things, walked with a drifty waver. I took her
right back and locked her into the fence. After a while, she
was attacking flies with her horns. She was in milk at that
time and so I threw away the milk as soon as I milked her
out. Three days later, a hippie friend came over and I told
him about it, let him test the milk to see if it had any effect. He said it didn't, so I went back to making cheese
and yoghurt. But for some time after that, I'd keep an eye
out for that particular mushroom and when I'd see it, I'd
trample it into the ground. Goats are as perverse as humans, when it comes to eating the wrong thing and getting high. Tree, like Sunshine the hen, loved wine and
beer. She adored cigarettes and would eat one in half a
second. I gave her a cigarette now and then, just one, if

she was suffering from bloat. It seemed to get her insides moving again.

She's been gone a long time now, but she enters my mind a lot. She's always welcome.

Notes

I find there are lots of people involved with animals in a similar fashion to mine, some sort of urgency, all trying to prove to the world that animals are people too. It's kind of a hard thing to prove because it is so fantastically obvious, that it seems that whatever is said is simply to look at that which everyone knows and say it in such a way that it becomes acknowledged.

PETER KUBELKA AND THE GIRAFFE

I keep finding more books about animals and all wonderful to me. There was one very recently about a quail named Robert who hatched in a house and saw people before anybody else and therefore gave them her heart, living there by daily preference like a dog or cat. Just today, I was given a book about dolphins, subtitled "a nonhuman intelligence" which made me think about a conversation I had with my friend Peter in which he was telling me about capturing giraffes in Africa.

When they go to catch giraffes in Africa, it is my understanding that they have figured several of those grazing animals out so that they chase them with jeeps across the veld but if they chase them at high speed for so many minutes, then the animals start dying from over-exertion, and so they've figured how many minutes for each species. They were chasing giraffes and they had about thirty seconds left, and they caught a half-grown female with the lasso and she was unharmed. Peter photographed it all and he photographed her face and tears coming out of her eyes.

Then she lay hog-tied on top of the truck and he rode beside her and saw her weeping all the way. When they got to the corral where there were other giraffes, they put her in there and she walked in dubiously watching the faces of the other giraffes but they came slowly up to her waving their heads gracefully and surrounded her then caressing her, sort of a high level jailhouse style. They surrounded her, it seemed, partly out of curiosity but gently caressing her to make her relax and feel content to join them. They surrounded her so thoroughly that for hours she was invisible from where the people stood.

Well, so I said that I knew that dogs were people and I knew donkeys were people, and I knew goats were people and I was happy to hear that giraffes were people too. Peter's simple but somehow thrilling reply was "Why don't you just say that people are animals?" The thing was, at the time – that was maybe three years ago – I simply hadn't thought of it that way. I was taking in the world piece by piece and thinking the rest, or most of the rest, was too stupid or somehow lacking in verve. I had been lucky enough to find a few really exciting personalities amongst the animal world, as opposed to the human world, to get to know. But from that time it seemed obvious to me that we're all in this together and, simply, we are all alive. What seems endlessly fascinating to me is to get some sense of the personal logic of some individual or other; whatever his life form might be seems only part of the logic, not really cause any more for discrimination. I guess I'm taking the word "equality" and pushing it to a place beyond politics where I can make the obvious statement that it isn't true that humans are in charge of the earth. The fact is, humans are one species that has specialized in a way very destructive to the rest of the life of the earth.

MESSAGING

Yesterday on television I saw where a man went into the lions' island in the zoo. It was said that he wanted to convert the lions to Christianity. In any case, the male lion, with the female looking on, hit the man with his nose, mouth open in a grumbling growl. The message was clearly stated: "Get off our island!" He didn't draw blood. The man stood still, seemed to be talking to the lions. He looked to me like a man led into the wrong place by a faulty idea.

Again, the male lion bumped him with his nose and the grumbling roar, this time taking the mans jacket that had been draped over his arm and tossing it to the ground behind him. At this, the man took a couple of steps backward and seemed to lose the strength in his legs so he sat down on a boulder. I think he had gotten the message. He seemed to be unharmed. I would have been interested to see what happened after that but the television went to other topics.

Now bears feel, like people do, that they own the world. In their case mainly it's the food. Why an excess of intelligence seems to lead creatures to such a blatantly inaccurate conclusion, I cannot for the life of me say. However, it is a fact that when people send savory smells out into the woods from a cabin with a flimsy door or window, it follows naturally that any passing bear would come for supper. And if, as was the case of this bear, the people had trained that bear to come to them for food; if, as was also the case of this bear, she had three cubs to feed, naturally she would walk right in – and take over.

This time I read in a book "Beauty Within the Beast" by Stephen Stringham, that a couple had a cabin deep in the woods with leather hinges on the door and delicious smells wafting out. I can imagine readers saying that bears should be taught to avoid human property and of course they very much do unless the line seems unclear. It certainly would to any bear in this case and if, as in this case, the bear was trying to raise and feed three bear cubs with just what she came across in the woods. This couple had been feeding this bear for years.

Any mother could understand what a godsend the smells from that cabin seemed to that mother bear. And so she entered the cabin, chased the owners under a flimsy table snarling so that she could go through the food, not only eating the meal prepared but also going through cupboards for more. Breakfast for two people is just hors d'oeuvres for four bears. She kept the people under the table until she and her babies were well fed. The way she kept them there was naturally by snarling and occasionally swatting at them if they moved. And deliberately missing every time: the swat a mother bear uses to tell the children to keep quiet.

When the couple emerged unhurt hours later from under the table, they fled from the cabin and never wanted to go back. And rightly so unless they wanted to invest in metal hinges and perhaps firm up the door itself and the windows. And stop feeding bears. Because naturally the mother bear would check on that cabin in her endless search for food for her cubs.

There was an old couple I heard about taking a walk in Rocky Mountain National Park and they came to a clearing in the woods. They saw a big handsome elk with a broad rack of antlers coming toward them, assumed that their status as humans would make him swerve from his course but he didn't. In fact, he came toward them, his upper lip curled up to show big yellow teeth, hissing. Elk weigh several hundred pounds each. The old couple backed into the woods and when they reached the edge of the trees, the elk left them, ran to the top of the clearing and escorted a female elk through the meadow past the wondering couple. They too called it an attack but again, like the bear, he had no intention to hurt them.

In all three of these cases, the messages were not what the people wanted to hear. The communication was of necessity scary and disruptive. But in all three cases the animal felt it was important to get the people out of the way – pronto – without hurting them. In each case, the animal was assuming authority.

None of these were attacks. They were demands. Communication.

The key here is the feeling of importance. All three of these messagings are completely understandable by any-one as totally "human" needs: keeping trespassers off the property, feeding the children, and the guy getting his girl. All that is needed by the humans in these cases is the understanding of the situation and respect for the needs and passions of other creatures, even though the other creatures' feelings are not protected by law.

Epilogue

I believe the lion and the elk survived having made their understandable demands. The mother bear of course was killed and usually in these cases the cubs would have been killed too but the author of the book, a behavioral scientist, spent the summer raising them in that cabin, using the skin of the mother to bring them in.

I realize that understanding their very "human" needs and wishes is not the point, particularly in the case of the bear. It was said that she would now be destroying human property all over the area and so, in justice, she had to have the death penalty. I see no way around this, but I know that it's wrong.

TYPEWRITER, SITTING WITH GOATS

To begin, then, on an ordinary day, for no other reason than that I have bought a sweet little ten-dollar typewriter. It is old and black and has two flaws which seem to me related. One is that the capital letters are not raised above the small letters, but droop instead below them and the other is that, from the same cause, the exclamation mark doesn't come off at all but looks like a colon and so this I will take as instructions to be mild and humble in my writing.

And so I begin.

This morning I lay for awhile with the two goats on the porch in the shade and, as they were quiet and chewing their cuds, I noticed again the feeling of sweet satisfaction and comfort that I gained from their company when they were doing that. They exude a pleasure in the workings of their bodies and an acceptance of whatever is around, so that when I am with them and they are chewing the cud, the trees and the weather and the birds are all as they should be and God's in his heaven. Tree tried again to climb into my lap but she is now six months old and weighs perhaps forty or fifty pounds. It wasn't so much the weight, I mean, I was willing; but I was just not big enough, and I endured as she clambered about on me as in the old days. Just a couple of months ago she used to sit for hours in my lap and chew her cud but now she has grown and now also I have a new typewriter.

Things change, and that seems to be necessarily the way it must be. She got behind me then and leaned on my head and I could feel her chewing her cud inside my head. Long eyelashes pointing down over her eyes, head held high on long neck, chewing, chewing. It got me thinking about giraffes. I looked them up. Giraffes have cuds, and furthermore they have in addition to their two horns, a third horn in the middle of the forehead which makes me think of the unicorn and maybe the unicorn was some sort of giraffe. I do believe in unicorns and dragons too, I mean that they were animals which existed and are now perhaps extinct, or at least the unicorn seems to be. Every once in awhile I hear of someone seeing a dragon or a sea serpent and why not, I mean if they're modest and retiring and prefer to be under tons of water, rising up only every century or so to turn some passing human daffy, why not? Just the most noticeable ones got vanquished like the mammoth and the cave bear, the giant sloth and so on, by those pesky pricking humans.

I see that although I have no exclamation mark, my question mark is excellent. The instructions are becoming clearer.

In the past couple of days, the hummingbirds have become very exciting, as two very different kinds have arrived at the feeders by the sink, sending me then to the book to look them up. I find the tiny rusty orange one is the rufous and this most common one is not the ruby-throat, over which Audubon went into one of his wonderful nineteenth-century ecstasies, but the broad-tail, which looks like a ruby-throat with an extraordinary tail. I don't know quite what to make of it, but it seems obvious that a Nineteenth-century ecstasy is much different from a Twentieth-century ecstasy, and both very different from a Twenty-first century ecstasy. We are so very much a part of our cultural time. I've noticed this in the various decades across my lifetime. The values change, and with the values, the goals and obsessions and passions are for different things.

THE OWL IN THE WOODS

Walking up the wagon road to the Magic Circle, just the dog Durin and the two goats Tree and Fawn with me, I heard a jay yelling, and yelling, felt eyes on me, looked up, saw a great horned owl framed in the branches of a dead aspen tree, he on the lower branch and the Steller's jay on the thinner branch above him. The jay was dancing and squawking; the owl was looking at me.

I looked back. Durin sat quietly at my feet, Tree and Fawn found a bush to nibble on, but even they were still and quiet. Minutes went by while the owl and I looked at each other. I felt honored to have his attention and I plunged into his mind as best I could. The face and body were still, in spite of the noisy jay above him. He looked at me, saw the quiet around me. And then to me it seemed that he told me everything. Except that I couldn't quite get it, certainly couldn't articulate it, but his meditative stoicism washed over me as though I was learning something grand.

The jay continued his yelling and dancing but never touched the owl. At one moment, the owl pivoted his head to look directly up at the jay, then back at me, seeming to say, "and, by the way, would you shoot the jay?" Then he spread his great wings and flew in front of me to turn and fly down the old wagon road where his wings wouldn't touch the trees.

We followed him and got to the Magic Circle, and I looked for him there, but I didn't see him; couldn't hear the jay, either.

The memory of that occasion and of our conversation, that I couldn't understand but could only absorb, has stayed with me all my life. Perhaps, I'm still absorbing it. Some learning takes time.

These three are animal stories in the book of local legends that I wrote years ago, now out of print, called <u>Lump Gulch Tales</u>. I collected the stories from the old people in the gulch who remembered the time in the 1930s when mining got serious again for quite a few years around here.

LUMP GULCH ANIMAL LEGENDS: The Fox Terrier, the Lion, and the Bull

Fox terriers tend to be squally, jumpy little pests for the most part, going into screaming hysterics if a cat or a neighbor walks quietly by minding his own business. Or they live with old ladies, jump for biscuits and get wheezy and fat with pink ribbons in their hair. But in their own way, fox terriers can be heroes.

Take mountain lions, for instance. What dogs do you think are best for hunting mountain lions? Fox terriers, no question. You take a dog like a German shepherd, a Doberman pinscher, or one of those brave hunting dogs, take a dozen of them if you can afford it, and hunt mountain lion, they'll go in and fight. One swat for each, that mountain lion will kill them all and get away. You go after mountain lion with fox terriers and those crazy little critters will chase her all right but if they get in sight of her, they'll be leaping about like popcorn, screaming in their squeaky little voices, and way out of reach. The cat may swat all she likes, she'll never hit a fox terrier. They're too chicken-hearted to get that close. Then, in disgust, she'll go up a tree.

That's what happened over beyond Nederland at the Van Vleet Arabian Horse Ranch, a registered Arabian colt got killed by a mountain lion and Jim Ryan went in there with fox terriers. People laughed at him when he started out but when he hauled that lion's carcass in with no harm to the pelt but one bullet hole and no dogs hurt, he got the last laugh.

The Merchants had a fox terrier for awhile. Young George had his head buried in the engine of a car someone had sold him cheap. This was in the late thirties. George was trying to get the thing working, had all his tools lined up, and was really now going to get it to go. The fox terrier was sleeping on the porch.

Mr. Green's range cattle were somewhere about as they always were. This year's bull was a particularly ferocious one, enjoying nothing more than chasing people, and fast on his feet too. He was perfectly all right if you were on horseback but not on foot. Big sharp widespread horns, he had. But one can't hide in the house all summer because there's a ferocious bull somewhere within five miles.

So George had his head buried in the engine of the car and suddenly that fox terrier started yelling bloody murder. George looked up and there, around the corner of the house, not four yards away, was that bull sneaking up on George, just taking another careful step, nose to the ground, eyes glaring up at him. Now George knew you should never run from a bull. That's the worst thing to do. But knowing a thing like that and thinking of something besides running when a bull is actually stalking you, well, the mind tends to wash away while you're running. George ran. But the fox terrier was so all-fired het-up barking and dancing around that the bull got distracted from George and started chasing the dog.

It wasn't six months later that little dog went out, with that special unbearable whine fox terriers use to express the sex-fire, and he never came back. George asked around but there was no one with a bitch in heat. "Coyotes got 'im," they all said. Probably did, too. Dogs come blindly to the smell, the coyotes know they'll come and ambush them. Fresh meat brought right to the pack, no need to hunt. It's a quick death.

But George remembers that little fox terrier fondly to this day. After all, he may have saved George's life.

LUMP GULCH ANIMAL LEGENDS: Handling Beavers

George and his wife Bonnie always had a water problem here, at least since they dug a well. When George was a kid and lived here on this spot in a log cabin, they just went down to the creek and there was always plenty. Actually it's only been since What's-his-name made his little fish pond up there some years ago that they've been having this trouble really bad.

When the beavers came back to the gulch, George and Bonnie were extremely pleased. It had been one of the pleasures of his life to have them here when he was a kid and when he and Bonnie bought this house on the site of the cabin he grew up in, the first thing he looked for was the beavers and they weren't there. Well, they bought the place anyway because they wanted to be near their folks but without the beavers it was sad.

Then, as I say, the beavers came back. It was the same year What's-his-name built his silly fish pond so you can't really know which did it to them. All I know is that winter they spent six months bringing water up from town, using the old outhouse and, when the drains froze up, unhooking the traps under the sink and putting buckets under.

It was rough but they got used to it and in the spring George decided to build a dam where he thought the water soaked in from and went to their well. So he joined the beavers out there, built this nice dam above theirs, and it filled up swell, deep enough to swim in. But then the beavers built upstream of it and it soaked away and the water didn't come down strong enough from their dams and the pond went pretty low.

So George started going out with an ax and chopping out the beaver dams to fill his, but those hard-working little buggers would fill in where he chopped quicker than it took to fill his pond. And he didn't like fighting them. He liked the beavers. A lot.

The next spring George thought what he'd do is to build a dam above the beavers and dig a trench from that down to near the well and fill up the well that way. So that's what he did, and it worked real good.

The only problem now is, you know how the young ones grow up and move along a creek, go up or down from the last dams, young ones grow up and have to build their own place. So now George is worried because so far they've just been eating the willows and they were moving upstream. But now that he built his dam above them, will they move downstream? And there's that patch of aspens down there below his folks' place, nice tall aspens, big around as Powerful Katrinka's arms. And you know, that's what beavers mostly eat is aspen bark. Well, you can't have everything.

LUMP GULCH ANIMALS LEGENDS:
From Henry Niccum

Henry Niccum found shelter where he could for free, so he'd live in miners' cabins above the old mining town of Gilpin. At one point, he moved to the shaft-house of the Alice. The Alice had been a good mine in the seventies and then it played out. A horizontal adit for fifty yards into the hillside, a fair-sized dump glittering lifeless but tantalizing in front of it and at the portal of the mine, smack up against the hole, a cabin, sixteen-inch thick logs, a little window on each side, a gaping hole at the back straight into the mine and a wide door in front for when the ore carts would come out on their tracks in the old days when it was working.

As it happened, Henry ran out of food about the time it started snowing and it came down thick for the rest of that day and all the next. So that when the third day dawned blue, Henry was mighty hungry and although the snow was over two feet deep, he set out to go visit Jim Murray because there was no future staying at the Alice with no food.

Molly Ball saw him from her house up well above as he was coming around the big curve and she watched him from her front porch as he slogged along, head bent and knees going up, arms swinging hard to twist his back around so the next leg could kick through the snow for the next step. It's a lot of work to walk through two feet of snow. Much better when someone has done it before you.

Molly didn't know he'd been through over two days without food but she did know something he didn't know and that was that some several yards behind him a mountain lion was mincing down his track. Even if Henry hadn't been deaf, there would have been little use for Molly to call out to him because he couldn't have gone any faster, there wasn't anything there for him to escape up or into and so Molly watched as Henry plodded laboriously along the long slow curve that circled around the peat bog and the mountain lion kept the same distance behind him and eventually many minutes later they both went out of sight around the next bend. It wasn't until days later she learned that he hadn't been killed, hadn't even known there was a lion behind him until she told him.

TIMBRE, WALKING WITH NEIGHBORS

Timbre had a way of loping tirelessly so that when we'd take a walk, she would make great circles of maybe one or two hundred feet radius around me and at the end of the day she'd be fresh as a daisy and raring to go. It was an ecstatic lope, too. In her eyes when she did it was a drunken laughing bliss mixed with an intensity of desire to know everything. She was a sensual one with a grace and endurance rarely to be seen.

She is really very pregnant now and though she is not due till August second, today I noticed that one of her breasts was engorged and I squeezed out a few drops of milk which made her yelp but then she felt better. I made a place in the kids' room for her to have her puppies. I put a board across making an area about five feet by three, laid out newspapers all over in there and covered them with a blanket (washable). Then we went to a movie so I left her in, but before we went, I sat in her place and talked to her for a while, she didn't come in then, but when we got back, we noticed that the blanket was rumpled, so that's good news.

Also I looked at her breast and squeezed out another drop at which she did not yelp, quite the contrary, she was having her belly rubbed, at which I theorized that a good mother would be one who liked to have her belly rubbed. This also developed from talking to the goat lady who said that goats will give milk sometimes in the spring even without kidding if you "stimulate the udder" as she put it.

This brought up that there is mention of the fact that in the island of Malta, they milk their goats differently. The goats there are petted and raised in the family rather and while they are pregnant, the goatherd massages the udder with greased hands often, then when they're in milk, instead of milking regularly twice a day like everywhere else, the goats go about town being milked by everybody all day long.

I went up the mountain yesterday with a couple of neighbor ladies who were very slow but that was fine. Saw a lot of flowers including some very weird star-flowered pyrolas and I found that a berry bush which I had noticed last week was definitely a husk-tomato or ground cherry which is quite exciting as they are edible and plentiful and if it interests me, they can be saved over the winter; I believe it does interest me.

I found to my immense surprise that my hut which I made last summer was in excellent shape. The only loss was that a lot of pine needles that I had put on the top to ward off rain had blown away in the wild winter winds, but I didn't mind because they didn't ward off the rain anyway.

I was surprised though to see that nobody not even in hunting season had written in the notebook that I left there, but the two ladies I went with kindly filled the gap. I didn't read what they wrote, but will do so next time I go up.

I have written before about the mountain and perhaps have the description too pat in mind to make a fresh clarity about it; suffice it to say that it is like an island in the sky, the slope coming abruptly to a large fairly flat or rolling island with one hill, the peak of the mountain at the northwestern point and my hut at the eastern point maybe half a mile or so away. Behind the peak is another half-mile or mile of island containing the cave and the lean-to ruins and the strawberry patch, all this to the south of the peak and somewhat to the west also.

Every time I go up there I get lost which is becoming a rare and precious phenomenon. I dearly love getting lost because only then do I have to see all around me as new and also it's a puzzle: how to find where I am.

After lunching in my hut, we went to the two cabins which are right on the edge of the island beneath the peak facing north, then to the top of the peak where we sat around trying to name things in the panorama, mostly with unsure success. By the two cabins is a mucky spring which I wouldn't like to use. While we were on the top of the peak, we saw a gray bird with black wings who hung around looking at us for a while in silence then solemnly opened its beak at which we all were hoping for a song in the clear mountain air but he let out a contemptuous squawk and then flew away. I haven't yet found him in the books but I will ask my brother.

On the way down then we stopped at Velvet Valley. Strange, I found every place they asked me to take them to. We sat around at the picnic tables there for a bit, surrounded by the smell of cow. I saw a washtub which I wanted for a winter flowerpot and tied it on myself with my scarf around my waist so that it was on my butt and flopped with every step.

What with that and the ladies having found driftwood we staggered incongruously on as soon after we left Vel-

vet Valley it began to rain in the most amazing torrents
with thunder and lightning very close. At first before it
rained I was plodding tiredly with my washtub on my ass
but when it rained, I became hysterical and went skipping
giddily singing tra-la-la-la down the path, the washtub
flopping wildly and the thunder and lightning glorifying
and the rain coming so thick that it poured into our eyes
and blinded us. I guess it was good that I got so silly as we
still had a long ways to go and one of the ladies had a
thing about lightning but she was so busy giggling at my
antics that it didn't amount to much. Actually, I love lightning more than anything and I imagine it was that that
made me perk up so. By the time we got home, I was ten
times over wet but still with my trusty washtub which
anyway I couldn't take off because my hands were so cold
I couldn't untie the knot; I sat naked for an hour in front
of the hot blast of the stove then curled up under the elec-
tric blanket for another hour and finally was more or less
warm again.

HUMMINGBIRDS, TIMBRE'S PUPPIES

It's been several days now and little has happened except people visiting, some of which was very nice and exciting, though exhausting me in a particular way, that is, I've become today very grumpy and stupid in conversation. I would like someday to speak of people with the same interest as I speak of everybody else, but for now, some terrible self-consciousness or political ennui dulls my senses despite all my interest and all my efforts and I must leave people out of my writings until this is corrected.

This morning, I went to fill the hummingbird feeders and just as I filled the first one and was holding it in my hand, a male broad-tail came and lighted upon the wire and supped quietly for a time then rose and with tail fully spread and bent under and with his full-throated male chirr he slowly circled my head, facing me all the time, taking about twenty seconds in the process. I stood still, not turning my head or even my eyes in his direction, feeling that if he felt like he was dominating me, as he seemed to be expressing, he would feel safer in my presence. So I stood with downcast eyes and his food in my hand wishing I could see out of the back of my head as at one moment he stopped for maybe a second behind me and I thought he had alighted on my hair though I didn't feel any weight. They never weigh as much as an ounce, though, and he may have done so. At any rate, he settled back on the wire and had another sup, though a short one, and perhaps just to be sure I knew he could he circled around again taking only half the time this time, and landed on a wire close behind my head. I believe he surveyed me. I stood quietly and after a bit he buzzed off so I finished my job and went in.

We have, as I was going to tell you earlier, at least four species of hummingbirds here at nine thousand feet. The thing that thrilled me and sent me to the book to look it up, was the arrival of a bright orange one, and also on the same day a species with longish feathers sticking out on the side of his neck. Always before, I had thought that we only had the broad-tail but a neighbor said there were five species here, which at the time I could hardly believe, but now I find that daily we feed at least three, the broad-tail, the orange one which is called rufous, and the one with feathers sticking out whose name I think is calliope. The rufous is a real hellcat, storming around, chasing all the other hummingbirds away with the utmost assurance though he hasn't yet come very close to me. They have a way of suddenly all of them having a passionate urgency to feed at one time and terrible fights ensue, though nobody ever seems to get hurt bodily, and always they spread their tails and chirr as I before described.

Timbre has had her pups now, eight of them. We all pretty much agreed that she'd have five. She had them on Crystal's bed. It was the only clean one of the lot. We collected some comfortable rags and put them in the corner. I knew she'd prefer one of the beds. Crystal was sitting with her petting her and Timbre was licking something and after a bit, Crystal realized it was a puppy so she hollered and we all gathered around. What a miracle, to be sitting there petting your dog and out pops a puppy, just like that.

Then soon there were two, and then four, then Stan arrived and was photographing the next two and by that time it was bedtime so I moved all the puppy scene to its proper place and the kids made all the beds and went to sleep. The next time we looked, there were eight, all strong and bright, not a runt in the lot, though I find some more interesting than others.

The miracle among the quantities of miracles related to birth that gets me, at least this time, is actually the one I guess that gets everybody at one time or another, that is how did she know so precisely what to do? She, you know, she pushed out the puppy and it was in a membrane bag and then she with passion burning in her eyes ate the bag and the kids were terrified that she'd eat the puppy but she didn't. In all the eight times she pushed one out, she passionately ate the bag and the placenta and licked up the blood and licked off the puppy and did everything just right and settled down proud and protective, resting then while her brood suckled all over her belly. "Instinct," everybody says "it's just instinct," and then they say, "We humans have replaced instinct with intelligence." Well, let me tell you right now, I don't believe a word of it and I don't intend to leave it at that. For one thing, according to my observations, intelligence is an abominable substitute for the incredible detail and precision of instinct and nobody, not even humans would make such a miserable poor choice. For another thing, I don't think humans in the slightest lack instinct, though there seems to be a great deal of embarrassment about it, and thirdly, in a nutshell, what in the name of god is instinct?

Well, I know that with people, when we have babies, we tend to want to have somebody with us. I know that the love of a mother for her baby is deep; it's instinctual. I think all the deep things are instinctual. Love and family and community; hate and war, too. Wanting to communicate with the family and the community is instinctual, too, and we have developed these wonderful languages. It's instinctual to communicate. Even unsocial species communicate. And part of their communication is verbal.

ROSY FINCHES

After four years in which I have listened to people in other gulches exclaim over the "beauty of the rosy finches", finally they have consented to grace the wire spool table on my porch. Lively creatures. Rosy bellies, they all look like they had gotten into my grandmother's rouge. The long feathers of wing and tail have white edges. The shorter feathers are brown to the head and on top of the head it seems is an indistinct patch of gray. They move together much more than any other bird I have had experience of, fluttering and swirling down onto the wire spool like a warm-blooded whirlwind, gobbling the seeds ravenously and delightedly with a single mind. I saw several eating with seeds stuck in the feathers of their cheeks, none ever straying more than a foot away from the others, the mass of them moving *en masse* as a single organism, with the cohesion of an amoeba, then flying off together at a sound from inside the house. I have noticed that juncos, though they come in large flocks in the spring, always have an eccentric or two who fly off in spite of the assurances of no danger from fifty of their well-meaning kin. But the unity of the flock of rosy finches leads me to think that such an eccentric could never occur amongst them, more's the pity.

I have the feeder on the porch this year, on the wire spool under the window, because I have always wanted it to be there. I believe that my reputation amongst the birds has improved enough that I will be able to get away with it. Pip the nuthatch comes all day long, that is, all four pips come and the Steller's jays come stealthily to the porch floor where pip kindly flings a generous amount of seeds. Also the chickadees are beginning to come, though I'm surprised at how seldom yet, but the snow is not yet very deep and perhaps there is a lot yet still in the forest. But then, they haven't got over their summer shyness; I must get some suet up soon.

MAGPIE MAMA

The magpies are scolding and scolding for hours and I don't know why. They're gathered in the meadow by the house and yelling at each other. Maybe there's a dead rabbit or maybe they're, yes, that's what it is, it's the adolescents, four full-sized, brilliant-plumed magpies chasing after a rather less brilliant but wiser-looking bird screeching and opening their beaks with wings half-open demanding their outgrown rights. She, patiently scheming to mature them, occasionally pokes into the open beak if it gets too bad, then walks casually but swiftly under the car, trying as yet unsuccessfully to ditch them. It's been going on for hours but surely in the end they will mature?

CHORES

Open my eyes, there's the sun on the flowerpot. "Must be eight," I think, using guilt and haste to wake up with, reach over and look at the watch on the windowsill. 8:15. Not too bad. Dress hastily, go to the kitchen for the milk bucket, set up the goat food, calf mix, bran, vitamins and a mix of bone meal and kelp. Out the basement door and they all start yelling, even little Daffy locked up in the car turned goat shed. Tree's nose hammers at the stanchion. I put the pan there and she's working at the food while I lock her head in, put the milk bucket up on the fence, gather the other two pans, climb over the fence (easier than unhooking the gate, walking through it, hooking it again), put the small pan of food in the car with Daffy, then Rose's food pan over the fence and into the other hand which is stuck through, ease it down to the ground for her over there. Back to Tree, her head locked in the stanchion, big black udder full of milk. There's the

lotion bottle stuck in the fence handy as I sit on the platform next to Tree. Lotion is cold, rub it around my hands
to warm it, mustn't touch the udder with cold hands.
Then rub it on her teats where it tends to be always
chapped, makes a good lubrication for milking, too. Place
the bucket strategically, i.e., where she won't step in it,
dirt won't fall into it, and aiming at it isn't too difficult.
And the meditation of milking, tsssss tsssss tsssss tsssss
rhythmic, staring at the fence or watching Rose eat, but
my right hand wearies before it's finished the job and I
have to milk that teat the rest of the way with both hands.
Tree gets restless finally and dances around. This year she
hasn't yet stepped in the milk, knock on wood, but she
does dance around. She's nine years old after all and
should be getting dignified by now. They live shorter lives
than dogs generally, so I was thinking maybe just milk her
as long as I can — one time she went for two years before
she dried up — then maybe let her retire from kidding. I
raised her in my lap with a bottle, held her when she was
operated on, midwifed for her when she gave birth
(though not this last time, I'm sorry, but she did fine without me. It would nonetheless have been friendlier).

Strip the teats then, roll the udder around like clay,
punch it a few times till I'm squeezing out nothing and
she's impatient. Move the bucket aside, at which point she

invariably snorts. I used to say "Gesundheit" but now I say, "Yes, dear." Fasten the lid on the lotion bottle, put it where it belongs in the corner of the fence tucked behind that little knot. Take the milk, climb up on the fence, hang the bucket on the hook where Tree can't reach it. Undo the hooks that are holding her neck in the stanchion while she throws her head around with all her might, supposedly to help, though it's a hindrance. There is usually a feeling of relating which is nice in that ritual, so then we both run to the car to let Daffy out. Tree ignores her daughter and cleans up the food pan. We all know I got all the milk already, Daffy doesn't even try anymore. Daffy and I traditionally talk to each other for a moment or two while Tree is eating Daffy's leftovers. Then the question of hay arises and I go into the garden for it, take a flake for Rose and one for Tree and Daffy, of course Daffy doesn't eat much yet. I see the potatoes in the old tires are dry but growing well, so I start piling more dirt around them, tucking it in, then I water them, dipping the water out of the big oilcan, the one I found in the woods, with the yellow bucket that floats on top. Each tireful of potatoes gets one bucket, quite a lot. Last year I hardly watered, and it was good, and this time I've planted them in tires and I'm giving them all this water. It's a dry year. Every year is another experiment, oh, will I ever learn anything? Leeks and onions in the cold frame, two buckets for them and one for the lilacs and one for each rhubarb. I must make a rhubarb crisp very soon, maybe mixed with an apple or two. The water, low in the barrel, getting rusty. I wonder how many years that oil can is good for. A few buckets on the compost heap (mostly chicken manure, very good, and, layered with straw, the smell went away in two days). Then I put the yellow bucket on top of the water, in the big can that's about empty now, hang the hose over aimed into the can, making sure that it isn't going to slither out when I turn the water on. Climb out through Tree's place where she and Daffy are now cuddled together back-to-back in the sun, take their water bucket, pouring any left over on the milking platform, open the gate to Rose's place, slip through, closing it carefully because Rose hates babies even though she's pregnant. I guess I'll give her babies to Tree if they're girls. So I first fill the buckets, sliding Tree's bucket down the fence with my hand through the fence like I did with Rose's food, while the hose is pouring water invisibly into the oil can, and I look at Rose's condition which seems like nothing is happening, very discouraging, toss a couple of feed pans over the two fences to be near the milk, which is still sitting in the shade, and wait for the can to fill. When the can is filled, there is the yellow bucket to tell me, dancing around on top of the water. The first time I filled the can, I left the can and left the hose in it after I disconnected the hose from the faucet and the water siphoned out through the hose until I realized it was emptying the can. So the routine is to turn off the water, pull the hose out of the oil can, then unscrew the hose from the faucet, and all that pours out is just the current contents of the hose, a quart or so and even that I use to replace what Rose may have already drunk, because we have only so much water, and when we use too much the pump makes a sick noise and we have to turn it off and wait an hour. I walk through the gate, hooking it carefully, climb over the outer fence, get the milk off the hook and collect the pans I've tossed over the fence. Put them in the bin. Take the milk up to the kitchen, get the little piece of cheesecloth that's dried after soaking in the chlorine solution and strain the milk into a sterilized gallon jar, put it in the re-frigerator. Wash out and sterilize the bucket and the cheesecloth.

Take the pot of pineapple mint that Mickey gave me up to the greenhouse and start watering things, check out this and that, the tomatoes, still green and growing, the comfrey, spreading like it was a weed, precious thing, the climbing strawberries, dying, why? Must be something in the soil. When I had them in pots, they did very well, now

when they have the whole trough to play in, they die,
dadrat them. Fig coming along, give it a slosh of water out
of the barrel, rosary plant, coleus, white Moses, jade, as-
paragus fern, wandering Jew, rosemary, kalanchoe, creepy
jewel, five kinds of mint, begonias tuberous and waxy,
grape, little peach trees, parsley, white sedum from
Goldie, green one from Mom, gray one from the LA air-
port, red one from the feed store man, very soon I must
make a gorgeous thing out of all those, plus the two I
bought for one-third price, twenty cents each. Pour water
into the sprinkler can and drip it lightly over the new lettuce coming up from seeds I saved from lettuce I had let
go to seed. I like to let things happen as they do (well, if it
doesn't get out of hand) and the nice lettuce wanted to go
to seed. I planted some of the seeds, dozens coming up
now in the tray I set up for them. Add a little fine dirt,
crunch the dried-up stalk of the mother lettuce into
crumbs, sprinkle that on the top, spread it as evenly as
possible all over the new seedlings, spreading as an after-
thought some kelp, and drench it all with water softly
from the sprinkler. Water the compost, the passion vine
and the polka-dot plant, the petunia and the Swiss chard,
the terrarium, the palm trees cautiously snatched from
the vacant lot in Riverside, California, before the bull-
dozer got there. I felt twice wicked, like I was stealing

something and might get caught and like all the baby palm trees in the lot were calling me, "Take me, too! Give me a chance!"

Some chance. A greenhouse at nine thousand feet altitude. Poor dears. Like living on Mars. Barrel empty, add a small slug of liquid kelp to sort of discourage the aphids, and run the hose, which drapes over the rafters and down, wrapped with enthusiastic thicknesses of the monster vine (will anyone ever tell me what Monster really is?), cut off a few flying strands. Once I let the vine go and he grew all over the ceiling of the greenhouse, shaded everybody, froze in the first frost after causing everyone else a great deal of stress, nobody was happy at all though he bloomed, and the flowers stank and strained him so that he was leggy — oh, the whole business was a mess. Passion buds aren't growing. And I fed it a lot of fish emulsion some time ago and the leaves look great. Tomatoes coming along pretty well. Some with green fruit, some budding first bloom, some leafing out, two starting up, just pairs of real leaves in with new lettuce, none of them planted, all volunteers. I quit planting them several years ago. Some fruit doesn't get found till it's past its prime or sometimes it lies on the ground like a marble and I see it there and don't pick it up, and in this way, over the generations, it's getting acclimated. Just the little cherry tomatoes. I've tried the big ones and they don't feel at home. They died young, brought sickness into my greenhouse. I like everyone to be healthy and beautiful. It's nice to have cherry tomatoes; I can pick one and eat it while working or collect a little bagful, fill a salad with the day's harvest. Why do they taste so good from the greenhouse? Maybe it's the soil or just that I don't pick them until they're red and eat them right away. No insecticides, of course, either. Bugs all over the place. Where are those chameleons? Whoops, turn off the water, it's overflowing the barrel; wooden barrel, when I leave it empty for more than a few hours it springs leaks and won't fill up for a few days. I stand awhile, look for chameleons, which elude me, soak up the emotions of satisfaction pouring from all my friends.

WORMS

But what I wanted to talk about really was worms. When you think about it, you can see that worms are perhaps the most ecologically essential animal in the world. Aristotle called them the intestines of the world. Charles Darwin spent the last years of his life studying them and writing a treatise on them. I think without them, we might be lost. Of course, the reason I got involved with worms is on account of my hopes and interests in a garden, and also on account of my failures, and successive reading. I have come across many references to worms: how to attract them, how to raise them in boxes over the winter, the care and feeding of worms, what to avoid if you want healthy worms, the sex life of the worm, etc.

Do you want to know the sex life of the worm? It's really very neat. They are bisexual, but, unlike the snail, I think they can't fertilize themselves but any two worms can fertilize each other. I remember cutting up an earthworm in college anatomy course and seeing that each worm has four separate hearts; of course we have four hearts too, but they're all stuck together. The sexual organs are in I think the fourteenth and fifteenth segments of the worm and what they do is facing opposite directions they fertilize each other then they both lay an egg capsule which contains ten eggs. These egg capsules are about half the size of a grain of wheat and will keep for months until conditions are favorable for hatching. The newly hatched worms are minute but self-sufficient and they mature in about three months so that they can lay more eggs. People who raise them in boxes in the winter have to keep adding more boxes every month.

The thing that excited me or at least startled me was one day when the ground was freezing, I decided to bring in the washtub full of dirt that I had outside so that I could plant my lemon tree in it and some other things and I was digging around in the cold dirt and there was a lump of worms. There must have been twenty or so and the ball was the size of my fist, all of them wrapped up together like the Gordian Knot.

As I hauled in the tub, I watched them slowly untie themselves and vanish into the dirt. I suppose they were that way for warmth. Now, as I have recently dug around in the tub, I find tiny white baby worms. Once I found them an eighth of an inch long and so thin they were barely visible to the naked eye, but they squirmed in just the inimitable way of earthworms and so now I'm feeding them there in the tub, giving them coffee-grounds and oatmeal. I must try to stop digging around in there to see how they're doing, because the book tells me that they really get depressed when their burrows keep getting disturbed like that. I wonder if I will have to get another tubful going before spring.

ROSCO

Once, I was enamored of an ass, a donkey, in fact slavishly, for the two years I had the honor of his presence. The people who owned him before had had five-gaited horses and one donkey who had, smart and curious and eager to try anything, learned to be five-gaited also, to prance with the horses, but then the two people had divorced; she had taken the horses and dogs and left him the house with Rosco the donkey, alone in the corral, and the deserted husband had, like an automaton, fed Rosco for two years until, one day, he sold him to me even though I didn't know how to tell Rosco to prance like he had learned to do.

Rosco, at the experienced age of fifteen or so, had been kept in solitary for those two years with no equine or human company and no exercise. He saw the sun and moon rise, cross the sky, set. Birds fluttered or soared or otherwise variously flew about him unpredictably. Cars and trucks whizzed by. Sometimes a walker or dog would pass, ignoring him unless he brayed. There were occasional butterflies. These things were never given short shrift by Rosco. Each one deserved and got full attention from him, the giant ears full high, the great soft eyes looking as though it were their first sight and then, ears back, head forward, tail straight out back, the deep, passionate, full-bodied roar.

Rosco's bray was not something that could be encompassed by calling it a "Hee-Haw" — it wasn't like that. The "Hee" part was a kind of a gasp, a strictured inhalation that seemed to say, "Here's something special," and the "Haw" part a great passionate roar. And yet, startling as it was and loud as it was, his bray retained a certain objectivity, so that although one might jump at the loudness of it, it wasn't an intimidating sound. Rather, it was a roar of somebody seeing something that was worthy of notice. And it suggested that perhaps he, too, was worthy of notice.

I kept him tied and had a little shelter against the house for him to keep out of the wind. I had no pasture or corral at that time. He was pleased with where he was placed because he could look down our driveway all the way maybe a thousand feet to the road, and see a lot of what was going on. It was early winter and he had a good thick coat of shaggy hair. He looked to me like a creature out of the far north, not quite a musk ox but definitely shaggy. I would stand at the kitchen window looking at him for silent minutes on end. He seemed so pleased with every little thing. I felt that having maintained that attitude across two years of being ignored showed him to be well-balanced and very wise. I realized that that reaction to loneliness was the wisest response imaginable. He had learned somehow to accept the life he got and live with it, emanating the love of his own existence and that of every creature around him, not being damaged by its limitations across those two years. I felt this as a great gift to me, a way around frustration, an attitude toward the day, the weather, the living things, whatever it was, that came within one's perception, to greet it as an equal, even to cheer it along if possible; to take everything that happened as a good thing in its own right. It amazed me that he had the strength of character to go on being interested in everything when he had been left alone for two years.

He seemed to me to be a philosopher. This recognition of every living thing makes everything valuable, shows each life as full of magical wonder, each event a glory. I have used these teachings with gratitude for the rest of my life.

In the spring, all his long hair fell out to reveal his short summer coat and also the snow melted and revealed a field of donkey manure. "What can I do with all of that?" I asked everyone, and someone answered, "Put it all into a pile and you will see that it will, across six weeks, shrink and transform into the best and richest garden soil imaginable." How I managed to not know this at the age of thirty, I can't imagine, but I didn't. "How does that happen?" I asked. "Microbes," he replied, "Little bacteria get to work and transform it across weeks." This was sheer magic. What an animal, to produce soil to feed my vegetables. I did as he said, shoveled it all into a pile and watched it across months as it slowly shrank, and then one day I went to it, picked up a ball of it, and sniffed it. It smelled like a lush greenhouse. Thus, I discovered microbes and working with microbes, and across years, I have seldom been in a situation where I wasn't working with microbes: making compost, bread, cheese, wine, conscious always of the needs of the microbes that were doing the majority of the work.

I was aware that he was getting no exercise on that rope and so I copiously felt obliged to ride him just about daily. The process was very simple. He had come with a bridle with a snaffle bit and I had very little trouble putting it on because he always wanted to take a walk. Then I'd take him over to a stump where I could easily get onto his back and that was it. I had almost no understanding of how to ride. We walked, mainly. I seemed able to stay on him when he trotted, but I preferred to walk because then I could see the world partly from his viewpoint. He took me farther than I had previously gone on foot. We found wonderful things, old cabins in disrepair, beautiful aspen groves, great boulders from which I could see the Gulch from a different angle. His ears fascinated me, working separately, long and seemingly very effective. I watched them in fascination. The left one would suddenly turn sharply to the left as the right one was straining forward; then maybe he would stop, head up, ears going, nostrils working, finding out what was going on. I dearly wished I could perceive what he perceived. There he was, obviously pointing with his ears to sounds beyond my capacity, sniffing things I couldn't smell. He showed me so much more than I could receive. It wasn't so much that I was shamed or frustrated by it; I developed a tremendous respect for him and his care and interest in the world that I barged blindly through, so that once as we would be perhaps approaching the top of a rise into an aspen grove that I had never seen, and he stopped, his ears going intensely, instead of kicking him to go on, I watched his ears to see what he was attending to. He waited. I waited. And then at one moment, he walked on and entered the aspen grove, empty now. I wish now that I had gotten off his back and looked for footprints, although I've never been very good at finding footprints. It did seem possible that he was just leading me on, but the tension of his ears told me that he was very interested and ready to bolt. I trusted him and waited. If he was going to bolt, I wanted to bolt with him.

Sometimes, if only to show that he was, in fact, a donkey, he would trot me over to a low branch that would, if I weren't attentive, have scraped me off his back, but I always saw it coming. Yes, he would have loved to run free — how could I compete with that? — but he did like me as a teacher likes his pupil. Whenever I have gotten onto a horse's back, I can feel the disappointment: "Oh, here's another novice. I thought she was smart until she got onto my back!"

When we'd get home, maybe I'd rub him down, or maybe just stand and cuddle for a little while, his chin on my shoulder, eyes drooping, lower lip flopping more and more as he reveled in being petted. Or he would press his head against my chest while I'd scratch him behind the ears and gently bump me with his nose. What a cuddly beast he was, and appreciated. He thrived on being petted.

One time, he got a piece of something very irritating in his eye and neither he nor I could get it out. It was really bothering him and his eye was very red, so I called Joe the vet. I knew Rosco would take to him, but Rosco had a way of jerking his head as an expression of demanding his independence, which could, on this occasion, have blinded him. So I held Rosco's head and petted him into stillness while Joe took the thing out of his eye, washed the eye out with something to heal it, and sewed the lids of that eye together to rest the eye. "Take out the stitches in a few days," he said to me as he left. So I did. Stan held Rosco's head and I took the scissors. "I can't go fast," I said. "You will have to put out hypnotizing sleep vibes." And so he must have done, because I cut each stitch and pulled it out by its knot and then all three of us held our breaths as Rosco opened his eye, and we all saw that it was a healthy eye and it worked fine. As we went back into the house, Rosco brayed his thanks. I leaned over the porch rail. "You are very welcome, dear friend," I said, so pleased.

One day we left early, I brought a lunch for myself, and we went together to the top of the little hill across the way. It wasn't that much of a mountain, but there were no roads up it and it took us all morning, going through the woods and meadows, dodging cliffs and rocky places, to get to the top. So lovely. We had a very nice time. But as we approached the top, a heavy mist came in and we struggled on, not knowing which direction we were going. At the top, while I was eating my lunch under a tree and he was grazing in a little clearing, the rain started down. It was a cold Colorado springtime rain and I wasn't dressed for it. In haste and blindly, at least I had no sense of direction, we went down the mountain, yearning for warmth and dry clothes, but when we got to the bottom, I saw that we had come down the other side of the moun-tain and here was the highway and seven miles to walk home along the road. This would have been fine if Rosco would have walked at a decent rate of speed, but he didn't. He went very slowly indeed, me alternately on his back kicking him to get him to go at a decent rate and jumping off his back to try to walk vigorously and warm myself up while leading him home, but he would go only at this very slow pace, mincing delicately along the road. Donkeys are known to be frustrating and during this entire afternoon, he showed me that this was also so in his case. The thing that I didn't understand was why he did it. I know, donkey owners would laugh and say, "because he's a donkey!" or "just to be contrary!" which fitted the character of donkeys in general but didn't touch on the actual personal motive. It is true that donkeys have a fear of running water. They are, after all, desert animals. It could have been mixed up with that. I had the feeling, though, that possibly if I had turned him around and aimed him the other direction on the highway, he would have taken me at good speed to a place where there were several dozen mules who worked hauling tourists into and out of one of the famous gold mines of Central City. I had watched his nose working wherever we went, and I knew he was yearning for creatures of his own kind every moment of the day. But I didn't want to lose my donkey, didn't accept rides offered to me in the rain. None of them could also carry a donkey. It took hours, but finally, in the endless rain, we got home, and I put him on his rope and went in to get warm.

Always, I was aware that the life I presented him with was not very satisfying to a donkey, and always I tried to make him content with the little he got out of this narrow life, but when I heard of a donkey race at Rollinsville, three miles away, I knew that he could beat any donkey they presented if he wanted to. So I walked him down to

Rollinsville and let a stranger ride him, but he didn't win the race because there, at last, were actual donkeys, and one of them was Buttercup and he wanted to be with Buttercup, so that no matter how strongly the stranger tried to make him go faster, Rosco just wanted to be close to Buttercup, who also was uninterested in racing, but wanted to be with Rosco.

The race was a farce. I should have known it would be. For me, it was a deep tragedy; for Rosco, a revelation of hope for friendship with a kindred soul, Buttercup. Somehow, I got him home, probably on the back of someone's truck, but after that, his patience with me was no longer there. There was no way that I could dominate him; I had to depend on his kindly behavior, but now, that was missing. He now showed me his spirit and his intention, and there was nothing I could do. One day, he got off his rope and I saw him galloping at great speed towards Rollinsville, where Buttercup lived. I found him in a pasture with Buttercup. He had been castrated years ago, but if any creatures could look like two creatures in love, it was those two. I crawled through the fence and stood there with them and they showed me how happy they were to be together. He even put his front hooves on her back as though to mate, and I understood what he was showing me, understood that he expected me to let him be happy with her. I knew he wouldn't treat me with the patience he had before, knew that he was a dynamic personality who needed to run as free as possible and to commune with his own kind. I can't imagine how he got into that fence. I wouldn't imagine he was any kind of a jumper. Maybe he found a low place and scooted through.

Sadly, I went to Buttercup's owners and asked if I could give my donkey to them because I couldn't control him now that he'd met their jenny. They said that would be fine; they had plenty of pasture and so I went home and that was the end of my time with Rosco. I worried some over the cold blizzardy winter when it came, asked the owner how my donkey was, and he said, "Oh, he was shot for an elk." And so I mourned again for that great spirit who had given me so much.

With the jawbone of an ass, Samson slew a thousand men. I yearned for Rosco's jawbone. I think it was a form of grief.

Years later, that man's son, Ken, told me, that his father was wrong about that. It wasn't Rosco who was shot for an elk, it was Buttercup, and Ken and his wife happily took Rosco into their horse herd and he went with them from summer camping to winter pasture for several years, but that one day, he walked away and they never found him, finally assumed that he had gone away to die.

When they told me that story, I felt confused, as though my friend had reincarnated and had a fun time for a few more years. And he deserved it; he was a grand fellow. But he had left me and he could have left them in a similar way. He could have caught a whiff of a delightful possibility. He had lost Buttercup. Horses would have been very satisfying. But think of the lone wolf howling and there was never an answer, then think of Rosco bray-

ing and never an answer, until one day, he heard a bray and followed the sound. He could always get through a fence, like a raccoon. Donkeys can live to forty or so. I knew such a one. His name was Tony. He was all alone in a little fence. I heard him bray once or twice at long intervals. I think Rosco walked away from that life with the horses to another life. Maybe it was those mules over by Central City. Maybe he found another jenny to live with happily for another while. It might have been a long while, or maybe he had other lives after that. He would have been right to live long. He had a lot of capacity.

A BOLT OF LIGHTNING

It was coming on toward twilight and a thunderstorm was moving in. I was sitting on the fence. I like thunderstorms. I looked to the west and saw that the sky was blue there. Where I was, a dark cloud hovered close down.

A bolt of lightning struck east of me, fairly close, and I looked up and saw it crackling. In the midst of the lightning was a much brighter shape, and when the lightning was gone the bright shape stayed there in the sky gleaming, as though it were a source of light. It sailed and flashed where the lightning had been, shining wings spread, slowly growing larger. It seemed an angel had been born and was filling out like a moth who had just emerged from its chrysalis.

Clutching the fence posts, I watched the shape, trying to decipher it. It sailed around in the same spot for a while until I realized it was the goshawk I'd been seeing a lot of lately, his light gray underparts reflecting the setting sun directly into my eyes like a mirror. He must have been startled by the bolt of lightning and managed to stay in the air by spreading his wings and gliding slowly downward until he recovered, thus appearing to my eyes to be growing. Goshawks don't soar much, they mostly silently flap.

After a while, he righted himself and I saw his dark gray back as he flew decisively northward.

SNAILS AND GUPPIES

I wonder if I can tell all the stories which revolve around the snails. One day a couple months or so ago, I decided to take the baby snails out of the aquarium and raise them in a pretty bowl I had bought, so I got some un-chlorinated water and I started gathering the snails. This has a few delicate rules to it, for though the snails are really hardy in many ways, they have weaknesses, notably that if you nick them hastily off the glass, they usually die because their suction arrangement is such that they've more or less got their guts on the line, that is if you mess up their suction, you mess up their guts. I have been able to persuade them off the glass, but it takes a little time. I guess snails have lots of time.

Finally after two or three days of biding our time and scouting amongst the leaves of the plants in the aquarium, we collected twenty-three snails and what with them and a few plants, the bowl was quite nice and lovely to look into. The only thing it lacked was movement, so I decided to put a couple guppies in there and I did and as soon as I did — that is, within the hour — they, that is, the female, was dropping babies all around in there. Talk about speed. The trouble with guppies, as everyone knows, is that they like the taste of baby guppy as much as anybody else does, so I took out the mate right away, left the female for a while. All the kids gathered around and Stan was trying to estimate the mathematics of it, whether she was eating them faster than she was giving birth to them, whether she was eating the weak ones that were slow or the healthy ones that wiggled more. Finally I put her back in the aquarium because I got to feeling grotesque with all that kind of figuring, but as I moved her the few inches to the aquarium, she dropped some in the net between the bowl and the tank and I put it in the bowl. After that there were new baby guppies maybe three or four a week for a month or so. I don't know quite how it worked but it may be that I only saw the few who escaped. Anyway, they all went into the bowl, of course, the bowl by this time was too populated and I gave away a lot of both guppies and snails, so that we were down to about a dozen of each and content with that.

There was one particular snail which came to my attention early in this scene. All the others were definitely in the shape more or less of a ram's horn, that is, a definite curl, but this one was different: streamlined, not sticking up, not tipping over, much faster, more energetic, seeming to dance in the water like an otter in extreme slow motion, not all that extreme, either. It was amazing how fast that snail could move along, with a pointed tail sticking out the back and a head like a horse, a curious horse, with those crazy antennae wobbling around, feeling things out and the head prehensile and nosing around everywhere, swinging that shell around expertly. Also when he was going fast and I saw him from underneath through the glass, he looked so much just like a penis. It was amazing, he was the same size and all as the other babies and I had to assume that he was a throwback to a recessive ancestor. You know, all the babies came from the single snail that came with a plant from the store, I mean there was only one parent, a real case of inbreeding, which happens often with snails. I kick myself that I didn't save him out into an aquarium just for him and start a new species of snail.

Well, two or three days ago, I noticed that the bowl had become some sort of unhealthy scene and began to change the water, seeing that it was too late for a few individuals, I did a rather thorough job of it. And yesterday, I noticed that although in the changing of the water, I didn't lose a single guppy, I had somehow lost every snail but the one, my favorite, and he was acting funny, so I with a feeling half guilt, half mystification, I fished out the corpses and kept them in a separate jar, hoping for one or another to quit playing possum but none of them did. After some effort, I persuaded my favorite to fall into a cup and be transported to the aquarium. It was one of those sentimental scenes when I dropped him into the tank and he did a stretching flip and sailed along the edge of a leaf; our pleasure was rather dampened at the sight of his dead parent back in a corner of the aquarium. Which left him alone, the only survivor of a terrible epidemic among the snails in our house. The death of the parent in the aquarium quite deepens the mystery, though actually, no care has been taken about spreading germs or whatnot between the two containers.

My favorite snail sits now as he has for days two inches above the waterline, only coming down at rare intervals to wet his shell, I suppose that in the end he also will die from starvation if from nothing else. This is important somewhat, because in this little snail, I believe I have detected an exquisite joyous spirit.

The kids took all the dead snails out to the front lawn, I told them they couldn't have the shells until the corpses had rotted out of them, so they put them on the ground, then, to protect them from god knows what, they built a mausoleum around them out of old bricks. This mausoleum is over a foot high and rather imposing, there on the front lawn.

THE DAY OF THE RUFOUS

for Jennifer Heath

July eighteenth and the rufous hummingbird came.
First time, no creature more exquisite, red copper iridescence about three inches long, five-inch wingspan, raising
havoc with the broad-tails — zeeoom — poor broad-tails,
one tends to think the broad-tails are nasty until the rufous comes along, then one sees obsessive nastiness. Such
beauty, vibrant, flashing gold/crimson! He'd never known
a feeder before, checked out the top, sides, seams, pulled
back to watch a broad-tail reach in the bee guard —
zeeoom — then immediately he knew how. So upset the
broad-tails were then, none could drink for more than a
second or two and he was there, chasing them off.

A female broad-tail was so upset that she came in the
open window where I was standing, went, naturally,
across the room to the big south window. I waited, hoping she'd go back out but no, she was sure that was the

way. I slowly closed the curtain but she dashed between the curtain and the glass. I had to open it and try again, pressing now the curtain with my hand against the glass. Her mouth was open; she was panting frantically, whacking and whacking that long, delicate beak, frail filament tongue against the invisible glass barrier. But when the window was completely covered now, she turned and flew up to the loft where the window, though open, was thickly curtained with a towel. I slithered up the ladder and across the mattress on the loft floor, reached up and yanked down the towel; she was out and gone in less time than an indrawn breath.

I leaned my head out and saw the rufous, such a jewel, dashing across the meadow — zeeoom — coppery ruby manned missile, to a point where he hesitated, perused the scene, then flew to chase off a broad-tail who had been supping on a flower — what a monstrous creature the little rufous is — my whole day has been like that.

DIRT

One time I had a flowering tree in a huge pot. It was a magnificent pot that someone had made in the shape of a goblet and three feet tall so that it held perhaps five or six gallons of dirt and stood between my side of the bed and the window, the top of the pot level with the windowsill.

I remember planting the tree, a four-inch twig with two or three lacy leaves and minuscule roots, on top of all those gallons of dirt, carefully spreading the dainty roots out in a sort of cone like one does when planting straw-berries.

It would have looked silly, that little lacy twig rising out of that stout clay pillar full of gallons of dirt except that, in fact, most of the pot was hidden by the bed and so it looked rather like an end table with a plant on it. And sure enough, characteristically, I used it as a table, put my teacup there, pretty shells, other things that wouldn't be likely to be hurt by getting wet.

One doesn't, if one wants a happy house plant, just stick it in any old dirt to prop it up. It's very difficult for creatures of our size to realize quite what dirt is, but after several thousand years of failing and succeeding and failing and succeeding, humanity has had to concede that if one wants to have a healthy plant for whatever reason, one has to provide that plant with what it wants in the way of water and temperature and sunlight and dirt. And of these four, no one can say one is more important to the plant than the others, because each carries the power of life and death. And so I carefully put it into that tall pot, pot shards at the bottom to hold a certain dampness after all else had dried, some of last year's compost, some soil from under the aspens and some from under the pines, more old compost, maybe a dash of bonemeal, some dead leaves, other stuff I can't remember. Gravel under the pot to discourage the slimy sorts of life, sunlight and lightness and air in the soil to encourage those microscopic lives whose gaseous effluvia we call "the sweet smell of spring-time." I tamped it down some, but not really effectively and then put in the little twig tree. It was called "the pow-der-puff tree." It grew fast. There in the big south win-dow, it grew in espalier shape, fanned against the glass, red puff flowers on it all the time. There was that pot of good dirt, there was the sun, the room temperature, and water/coffee/tea/various encouraging liquids, baby earthworms I gave it, and it throve magnificently, smiled joyous vigor out the window at visitors for I think about four years and then very suddenly it died.

The goblet-shaped pot fell apart when I tried to pull out the corpse and in doing so revealed its contents: not the gallons and gallons of dirt I had put in there but clean, bare, flesh-colored, finger-thick roots entangled into a goblet-shaped knot. No speck of dirt left except the top two or three inches which hadn't in those four years moved or buckled or risen or in any way, revealed that below that thin layer, that mask, the rest of the dirt was being consumed, transformed from handfuls of loose crumbs to that magnificent unity of enthusiastic life that lay now dead on the ground, just beginning the inexorable transformation back to the separate, dark, sweet-smelling complexity of millions of interwoven and ever-changing lives that we call "dirt."

THE RAVEN

The raven was definitely going somewhere. It wasn't just that, though. The way he moved was not only regal, it was beyond pride. He went across the world with a slow muscular roll of his wings, neither hunting nor fleeing, seeming aware of everything below him (including myself) yet unaffected, minding his own business without blocking out any knowledges or trying to change anything. And as I say, he did speak, I think that possibly there were three of them, and they were talking amongst themselves. It was years ago and my memory of the particulars has given way to the essentials. He (or they) spoke and in the speaking was carried the same impression as in the flying; it was of course what is called a croak. Laugh if you will, dear Reader, but in that sound was carried all the grace and grandeur which I have tried to convey to you about the manner of his flying. Ah, well, words fail me. All that happened was that a raven or maybe three ravens flew croaking across the sky. It was a matter of a few seconds and he or they vanished behind a hill and left me standing below in raptures of helpless admiration, I wanted then to fly and I wanted to make friends with a raven. I am reminded of a song my brother used to sing, "I must know what the wild goose knows, and I must go where the wild goose goes." Only these were definitely not geese. They were ravens.

WITH BOBO AND THE GOATS

A beautiful morning. I awoke with the urge to go up the mountain to my hut. I was the only human in the house and it was easily possible to leave. I took the two goats and Timbre the dog. I packed my knapsack full of stuff: bananas and candy and cheese and gloves and socks and a bit of rope and a recorder. And some rhubarb and ginseng seeds I thought to plant up there, along with about half a gallon or so of compost to give them a bit of a start. I wore my great heavy hateful insulated marine boots and I wore two shirts with a sweater and I brought along tied around my waist a jacket and a large shawl and my homemade fur hat and a canteen full of water and a bowie knife, and thus attired and in the aforementioned company, I went clattering and thumping along, feeling really grand and sparkling.

As we started out, I saw my dear friend, the neighbors dog Bobo, skulking along behind us under the shrubbery and behind rocks, peering at us over branches and from around tree trunks in the most amusing way. Finally, when I was afraid he'd go home in despair, I hollered out that he was welcome to come along if he wanted to, and pretty soon he eased up a little closer and I heard him trotting behind me, going fast enough to pass me, so without changing my pace or turning my head, at the proper time, I reached out my hand and felt his teeth gently bite the tip of one finger as he went by. God, what a clever romantic he is.

So we went along at a rather slow pace, my main effort being to walk where the snow was shallow, which was not very hard at all as the winter had been so mild and sweet that there was very little snow now and even the drifts were only two or three feet deep. Finally we came to where a snowmobile had been and we found that the tracks held us up on top of the snow, so we went with good speed right up to Velvet Valley without stopping at all, just walking slowly and looking and smelling and listening and laughing together and I would reach down to touch the back of whoever passed me.

At Velvet Valley I sat and leaned on a stump and ate a banana and gave the skin to Fawn, then both goats began nosing violently in my knapsack and I had to shove them off. I sat awhile and then I thought to plant some rhubarb there in the sun, so I took out the seeds and the compost, got out the chisel I had brought for a trowel, dug a little hole wherever the dirt was soft enough, replaced the dirt with a handful of compost, put in two or three seeds and didn't cover them very deep as I remembered reading somewhere that rhubarb shouldn't be planted deep. As I was planting the rhubarb, the wind suddenly came up and the sun went behind a cloud and I looked up and saw that the whole western sky was clouded over and that the wind was coming from there. A snowstorm had already reached Arapaho Peak and James Peak and would soon reach me. I hastily put on my jacket and my hat; planted rhubarb till I ran out of compost, ate some candy, drank water from my canteen, put on my gloves and skipped back down the snowmobile track. I had to stop my frenzy and calm down because I had spooked the goats and they were skittering and baaing and chasing the dogs and acting generally as though they were ready for a stampede through the forest. I didn't have to speak to them but once, and other than that it was just a matter of vibrations and was easily handled, as I wasn't really afraid of the snow and the wind. We went on downhill at a good clip and merrily enough, the dogs running in circles around

me and the goats. One time Bobo came galloping up behind me, forgetting for a moment that the goats would
misunderstand his hilarity and either bolt or attack him.
At top speed he came up behind me and remembered just
in time, slamming to a halt and swerving off the snowmobile track at the same time so that he buried himself up to
his shoulders and had to clamber backwards to get out of
the snow. He was so comical that I laughed till he growled
and ran off behind some trees.

Notes

The long story of the great dog Bobo is in <u>The Lady Orangutan and Other Stories</u>

AN ECCENTRIC CHICKADEE

There's this one black-capped chickadee that goes down the hole in the middle of the wire spool where I put the seeds these days. That's really something, if you think about it. Must be dark in there. But you see, I scatter seeds all over the top and of course lots of them fall through and into the center which is all metal — really just a big tin can — with wood going out from its top and bottom, serving as a table on the deck. The wood has a terrible surface, all crags and holes and splinters, for which I'm very grateful now with all this wind blowing these days. Actually, I think I'll encourage the kids to carve their names in it and whatnot, because the seeds stick in the cracks. The only place else they stick in the wind is to bird shit.

The wire spool sits right under my window where I sleep or read and as I sit there, I see this delightful black-capped chickadee arrive at the spool, look around with a look; yes, an excited smirk. Not a smirk on his beak, of course, but all over his body, his movements like someone having a secret love affair with a movie star or someone, to be more precise, with the key to the cellar.

So he looks around a bit, maybe coyly picks up a seed or two, then flies to the edge of the hole, looks around again, then plummets down the hole. At first, there was some difficulty in getting out, as the hole is smaller than his wing span. He would struggle up through the hole with a treasure in his beak, look wildly around in fear and trepidation, and escape pell-mell to the comparative safety of a nearby tree. But after much practice he has become very adept, sometimes actually flying through the hole and off to a tree without stopping at all, looking like a cannonball with wings.

The suspense is awful after he goes in. Nothing, you know, silence and emptiness. I put my book down and fidget. I imagine it's like when a whale is sounding and the appearance of nothing is so blatantly incorrect. And there are dangers. He might, of course, misjudge his direction by an inch and crack his head, break a wing, choke on a sunflower seed, and I don't believe I could reach my arm through that hole and down to the bottom to retrieve him. Then, of course, somebody might arrive on the top of the wire spool: a Steller's jay, a dog, a child, or a flock of rosy finches. I don't really see why the rosy finches should bother him, except there are so many of them.

Notes

As I was writing <u>Lump Gulch Tales</u>, many
people in the neighborhood thought of stories
to tell me. A good story is good to pass along.
They were all based on truth, I have no doubt,
and this one, in particular, was told to me by
the three people involved on separate
occasions.

Since I ran with dogs as a child, and then
when I was in my teens, I wanted to write a
dog dictionary but I couldn't think how to tell
completely how a dog was expressing what he
said, I had given up in despair.

This story about these wolves, was very
important to me and I kept trying to tell it
from different viewpoints. This was the best
of my attempts. Until I realized that here was
my chance to make a book that would answer
my wish for a dog dictionary. One problem
with writing such a dictionary was, in this
case, I had to learn about wolves and
everyone they interrelate with: deer, rabbits,

*ravens, coyotes, bobcats, pika, a whole ecology
of creatures. I have lived in that ecology most
of my life, so that helped, but I felt I needed to
read and understand dozens of scholarly
works, preferably interspersed with anecdotes,
about all these creatures, so that I could write
a dictionary of wolves, of wildlife. And so I
did that, and gleaned lots of detail and lots of
acknowledgment that what I had found
during my earlier years was right.
This, Elsie's story, is the story that <u>Wolf
Dictionary</u> came from, and I give deepest
thanks for it to Elsie and Mabel and Yukon
Jim.*

ELSIE'S STORY OF THE LAST WOLVES

I came back up here to Tolland to die. I love it so here. Here was where my husband and I were happy and after he died and then so many cancer operations on me that there was no more they could remove, even the medical profession gave me up and I crawled back to die among my memories. I have our little house, overlooking the big meadow so full of ghosts for me. I can see with memory's eye the work going on there, the mill on the left, the hotel, the saloon, the post office, the men going back and forth, swearing and sweating and bursting with their lives. Now, even the buildings are gone and the meadow lies empty to the casual eye.

My husband was an engineer on the D&RG. I won't go into our happiness or the dismal deadly sorrow I felt when he died and the cancer that soon tore into me. Now with my breasts gone and only half a lung, I came here to the place where the mountains and the weather and the D&RG are my neighbors. One's life is one's loves. I found that the place I crawled back to to die brought me back to life and has in itself filled my old age to overflowing.

For one thing, there are the trains and all the dear old friends running them. Whenever they approach Tolland, they blow their whistles and I must come out on the porch and wave my handkerchief to say hello and tell them I'm all right. Therefore, I'm never lonely here and my husband's friends — my friends — come by and say hello several times a day.

I read a lot — I love spooky stories. Ghosts. Frankly, my life revolves around ghosts and reading about them reassures me. I never get scared reading those stories; I just believe them.

That winter promised to be interesting. Yukon Jim was staying in the little place behind mine, and Mabel decided to come up too. And that was it. It was just the three of us, each with a little cabin for privacy. It was when I had just come up the mountain to die. I think Jim and Mabel came to watch over me so I wouldn't be found rotting in the spring thaw. Pretty flimsy help, really, but what help did I need? I was dying or we all thought I was and there was nothing anybody could do about it. Mabel looked solid and strong but her legs were giving her a lot of trouble, poor dear, and a lot of pain. Mabel is a really good sort, you know, basic and down-to-earth — warm and thoughtful. I was glad to have her there as I imagined my deathbed scene. She'd know what to do and she wouldn't get hysterical about it.

Yukon Jim was another story. He was one of my suitors way back when, though he never stood a chance with me and I was clear about that from the start. That never stopped him, though. He's one very smart man, I've never denied that, but I can't stand the weak-willed way he drinks. He has stuck with me, I will say that for him, and with his good brain when he's not drunk, he's really nice to have around.

There we were then, the three of us, feeble to the point of silliness, no car; none of us could drive, anyway, but some friends came by every week or two from further on up the road and took us down to Rollinsville to get groceries and our mail so we weren't cut off. And I know everybody around was placing bets on how long I was going to live.

We all stocked up, you know, lots of beans and such. The first snows came and then when the road closed, we settled down. I had a good stack of spooky books to read and it was really peaceful, collecting firewood, eating, waving my hanky at the trains, sitting around in the late afternoons with Mabel and Yukon Jim to look across the valley and chew the fat, then getting into bed to read about ghosts. The winter wasn't far advanced when we first heard the wolves. That was really something. What a sound. I mean, we were just sitting there on the porch and Mabel was talking about something and I heard it, I mean the howling. I guess it was because of listening for the trains, I heard it off in the distance lonesome and deep and mysterious and it was a lot like a train whistle that way but even more so if that's possible. Maybe a little like a ghost too, you know? It's a sound a ghost ought to be able to make. I'm sure it would be very satisfying. Then another howl a little closer.

I was very excited and I just went in and got some table scraps and put on my boots and everything and took those scraps out and dumped them down there below the tracks. I thought maybe the wolves would find them there. Next day I went down to look and sure enough, the scraps were gone. I don't know why I was so pleased but it just gave me a new lease on life. Really, I just felt a lot better then, stronger and cheerfuller and easier breathing too.

Matter of fact, I really got involved with those wolves. They were so romantic, so loving with each other, and they were wild and free and yet they were terribly unsafe, the last of a powerful breed. But they played together and loped together after rabbits or just for the heck of it across the meadow and as they ran, they looked more graceful than anything I'd ever seen like they were angels flying low. They brought tears to my eyes many times as they would cavort together and I couldn't help thinking and comparing them with my husband and me in the golden years of our life. It was a revelation to me because then I knew that golden times were happening still, even though they were not mine, I could see them and recognize them and they warmed me. They warmed me as much as the ghosts do and for the same reason. Oh, dear, I don't know if I'm saying this well.

Anyway, we watched those wolves and loved them. I think with my excitement over them, Yukon Jim and Mabel caught it too and they were watching as avidly as I was. It was a wonderful time we had then. The wolves were coming every day for our scraps and then we were watching them run and play and work and search for game and sit around in the sun and dig in the snow and nap together under a tree. We saw what they thought of the weather by how they carried themselves, we saw that they thought their happiness would go on forever. Of course, I knew better from experience but even I felt the enchantment. At least I thought it would last the winter, for pity's sake.

Every day they were there and then suddenly they were gone. Just like that. It made me sick, literally. I could hardly get up the strength to wave my hanky at the trains as they went by. I just sat in my chair by the front window all bundled up in a blanket and looked for them. Jim and Mabel were worried too, just as worried as I was, more so because they were worried about me too. So we all just looked for them all the time day after day. Actually, it was only ten days but you know how that kind of thing can feel like forever.

At last, I saw him. I knew it was him because he had a crooked ear but he looked miserable. Right then I knew what I had already known, that the golden time was over. Poor old wolf, I cried when I saw him, I knew so well how it was. He was thin and drawn out and draggy, just like I felt when my husband died and he sat at the edge of the meadow in the twilight and mourned. Of course, we all three got a pile of leftovers to feed him and all and he did eat a little but he was so sad, it broke my heart but there was nothing else we could do. I finally didn't want to look at him but I couldn't stop. It was like that.

Then when he took up with that female coyote, my blood started running again and everything looked up after that. Oh, it wasn't like it was with the wolf's real mate, but the coyote was a sweet little thing, rolling in the snow in front of him and flashing her bushy tail around. She was really young and playful. We could see how he warmed to life again with her and a new kind of good times were with him, more quiet of course with a sort of deepness underneath.

After that, they were always together. Jim just happened to have brought up a pair of binoculars when he first arrived and we really used them a lot. We sat there on my front porch and just passed them around and around. You could see expression better with them and details. I remember in a story out of the Greek myths where there are three old ladies way out in some wilderness with one eye between them and one tooth and one something else, I don't remember what and they kept passing these things around. I always thought it was a pretty goofy thing, you know, just unbelievable, but it always haunted me too.

Somehow, it was nice and I liked to think about it and one day as we were on the front porch, passing the binoculars back and forth, I realized we must look just like that, sitting up here in this wilderness, Mabel and me and Yukon Jim, passing the binoculars around and around, watching that wolf and that coyote living their lives. I can't tell you how funny it was when I thought of that old myth. It was funny for days. It's still funny. Well, funny isn't really the right word but you know sometimes an important idea will come along and I just have to laugh or something because when I thought of those three old women, I knew it was kind of wonderful to be old and decrepit. You know what I mean?

The wolf and the coyote were so nice, really. She went all out to make him happy, so playful she was and his face, which had been really tense and droopy, started looking tender and pleased. I don't know why people say animals don't have and express feelings like we do. It seems obvious to me they're just as different from us as we are from each other. All I have to do is look at them just like I look at people and I can see at any moment that they're having some emotion or another and I know more or less what it is. I'm sure anybody can do this. It's one of the most basic and important forms of communication, just the way one carries oneself. Why people won't admit to recognizing it in animals is a mystery to me. We're animals, aren't we? How can anyone doubt it? Well, I didn't mean to get up on a soapbox about this but I think it's just the silliest thing the way people won't acknowledge the obvious and when I think of that wolf and that coyote just warming each other's souls out there in that meadow, well, it was lovely beyond describing.

After a few weeks, it seemed to me that the little coyote was beginning to "show," as they say. Mabel was shocked at the idea, partly because they didn't seem to be the same species but mainly because of the size, you know, the puppies would be enormous for her. So we worried and talked about it and passed the binoculars around and the days went by.

Then one day the wolf came alone and we all looked at him and we thought maybe the coyote had died bearing those cubs but as I looked at him carefully through the glass, he didn't seem depressed but the days and weeks went by and we never saw her and it was really suspenseful, combing the mountain looking for a den, looking at the wolf to see how he felt. Really, he just looked fine and hardworking and he ate everything we put out there then he trotted off and into the trees across the way so I guess that's where the den was. You know how they feed their cubs. They eat a lot and then they go home and throw up.

Honestly, life is just amazing. Anyway, we wanted so badly to see her and the babies if there were any babies or whatever but it was over a month that it went on like that, him coming and eating like a horse, then going away and coming back and going away again. Jim got discouraged and decided she must be dead but I never thought so, not for a minute. He was too busy. He was too cheerful. I knew him well by that time. He would have sagged and drooped and felt bad. He would have looked lost like he did when his first mate died. Instead, he looked like he knew just what he was doing and why.

It got to be a very close thing at the last. I had to get to Denver by a certain date. Mabel and Yukon Jim had to leave too. The long winter was about finished up and we were all packing everything to go away for the summer. It was really bad to leave that lovely lonesome place with the wind and the snow and the mountains and the trees and rocks and rabbits and the birds we were feeding. We had enjoyed each other's company too, as we all watched the last wolf and his struggles for life and love. It was the wolf that was really getting us — not exactly the wolf but the coyote and mainly the cubs. We wanted so much to see whether there were cubs, what they looked like, every-thing we could and day after day, we watched for her but only he came, frantically eating and quickly trotting away.

So we finished packing and we had the one evening left and they were going to come and get us in the morning. We had about given up on it. We were sitting on my porch drinking tea and eating some cake Mabel had made when it just happened. The little coyote trotted over the snowbank. Then she turned her head and looked behind her and waited a few seconds. We were all on tenterhooks, you can imagine, and then the cutest face you could ever believe rose up over the snowbank and there he was on top and then tumbling after his mother as another face rose up over the snow and another until there were four of them altogether all bumbling around and playing and falling down at their mother's feet and just generally a happy, healthy litter of puppies if I ever saw one. And four lovelier babies no one could wish for.

We went to town next morning feeling fulfilled. We had things to do. I wanted to show the doctor I was still alive. Now I'm back here in my cabin, I feel like I see the wolf sometimes out of the corner of my eye but I honestly think it's his ghost. Lots of times, though, I see wolf-coyotes all around here. I don't know why they look so strongly like wolves still, years later. Maybe that wolf is still back in there or another one. I feel so proud about those wolf-coyotes. Like a grandmother.

Oh, it was a lovely winter that year and now I'm back in Tolland for good. Everything's more or less the same though a family has moved in now down by the tracks and Mabel feels the need with her legs so bad to stay in Rollinsville. Yukon Jim has moved to Central City where he can drink all he wants. Some young folks moved in to one of the cabins last year. I could have strangled their dogs, chasing off if not eating all my tame squirrels and rabbits and birds. The cancer hasn't come back yet. Maybe it will, but the main thing is the trains still toot for me and I still wave at them with my hanky and I still read spooky stories and look across the tracks at my ghosts. Among them now is the wolves and the coyote and her lovely cubs. I sincerely believe that they saved my life because they gave me joy. And Mabel and Jim, too, of course.

MIGHTY MOUSE

It began with one of those grade school projects where the teacher buys two dozen fertile eggs and incubates them and breaks one open every day to show the children how the embryo develops. The first few days, the eggs seem to get more and more yukky and then gradually across a few days one can see the growing purpose, the unfinished bird stopped in early development there in the dish before the children. The closer they are to full-term, the longer they take to die, but they're only eggs, after all, to make omelet out of, or pumpkin pie. One hundred million possible chickens out of each egg, the rooster's sperm speeding with rhythmic intensity toward the goal, each sperm's purpose to touch it, enter the egg and merge its individuality with the individuality of the egg, making an individual and never-repeated chicken. But life is so fulsome. There are enough chickens in the world, even with everyone eating them so much, two over

easy, a chicken in every pot, chicken soup with rice, buf-
falo wings, Cacciatore, etc., all across the land. If we didn't
eat them, they would be made into dog food like the
horses were when the car came in and replaced them.

At the twenty-first day there were three eggs left in
the incubator and the fifth graders watched in awe as little cracks and holes appeared in the eggs, took turns
bending their heads down to hear the tiny tapping of the
chicks still in the eggs pounding with all their little might
to get out now of the shell that had kept them safe and
alive so far. If they didn't get out this day, they would suf-
focate and die, so they had to have a certain amount of
strength and determination.

The littlest egg broke open first, before lunch, and
there drooped a soggy, exhausted creature, his bulging
belly still showing the workings of his digestion through
thin gray skin lightly streaked with sparse wet down. His
bare, three-toed feet couldn't hold him up and he sagged
there amid the shards of his shell and all the fifth graders
thought he would die like the others had.

But he didn't die. And the two other chicks hatched
out before the end of the day and Cheri said she knew a
lady who was raising chicks and could take them and that
lady was me.

I put the three in a box separate from the Leghorn chicks I was raising because the Leghorns were considerably older and looked monstrous next to these newly-hatched infants. The one from the littlest egg grew but was always the littlest. Soon, he revealed his masculinity by growing a comb at the same time he was growing black and white striped feathers. Unlike the other, bigger chicks, he seemed unafraid of our hands and would even climb up on a hand, stretch his neck and look into our faces. We named him Mighty Mouse for his bravery and his small stature.

Soon, we put all the chicks out in the chicken house where the three or four older Rhode Island Reds could see them but not peck them and they grew, then I released them into the yard. One of the Leghorns was a rooster too and I watched them as, instead of fighting, they became buddies together. Mighty Mouse, less than half the size of the other, proud and yet amiable. The two would crow together, answering each other from across the yard.

The other two chicks from the school project grew to be fine full-size hens, one black, one brown, but neither one lived long. The black one I believe was killed by a raccoon named Alice whom we raised then later released. Alice would come back to visit sometimes, leaving a partly-eaten chicken as a calling-card. It was a devastating time for the fowl that next spring when Mighty Mouse was a year old.

There were about a dozen chickens roosting in the chicken house and one hen, Sunshine, on the porch. Sunshine was lame and had suffered so much at the beaks of chickens that she would not live with them again so she roosted in a box on the porch.

There was a great deal of peace and harmony, cheerful scratching and clucking, the white rooster crowing with enthusiasm and Mighty Mouse answering amiably, "All's well," from two places in the yard. There is something particularly sunny and sweet in the sounds free chickens make in their daily tasks of finding food, laying eggs, and keeping track of one another. There's the contented murmur of hens feeding which sometimes the rooster will speed up and accentuate to a rapid-fire enthusiasm. When he's found something good and plentiful, he makes a special call and the hens run to him and they will all peck and scratch together for awhile, gathering close around him. There's the ecstatic song of success a hen makes, when she's laid an egg. Sometimes the rooster will join her in duet. Sometimes the whole flock will sing together in chorus to celebrate the goodness of a day, the happiness of being together and the joy of life. Chickens have a lot of emotion, they're sensitive creatures and, being social, they have many forms of expression. Song, tone, stance, style, distance, speed, angle, personal relationships which sometimes change. A laying hen, her comb deep red and full, her stance proud, has a place in the world, work to do. A hen on an off-month, not laying, her comb pale pink and withered, keeps her head lower, is more wary, her song is often a grating growl of warning. She pecks her inferiors and is pecked by her superiors. Life is one tenterhook after another. She keeps more to herself, doesn't join in group singing, looks to find comb-reddening egg-making food for herself somewhere.

Mighty Mouse's crow did not mature for many months. This was, I suppose, a necessary ploy to keep his secondary position, probably his life, intact. The white rooster, at a few months of age, learned to crow with the full barnyard sound, very satisfying to hear. But Mighty Mouse's crow stayed half-finished, as though he was not full-grown. It was a cute crow. We humans liked to hear it and we would smile at how cute it was. Anyone could know to hear his crow what place he'd taken. He seldom crowed until the other one had done so and then he would answer. But he stood at his full height, small as he was, held his head very high and I could see his eyes looking at things, judging, figuring, treasuring the attitudes of every living thing around him. Unlike all the other chickens except Sunshine on the porch, he trusted the family of humans who lived in the house and let us pick him up and pet him, ate out of our hands, even crowed in our arms. He was not fearless, his eyes were too intelligent, too busy watching, for that. But he was very brave. He made quick judgements and lived by them. And he loved grandeur, loved a good show.

Sometimes, in spite of the fact that Sunshine was terrified of chickens, Mighty Mouse would visit her on the porch. Sunshine never left the porch; it gave her a certain distance from the chickens, a height above them, and a territory that was her own. The ground slopes under the porch so that on the north end are three steps going to the yard and on the south end, a sunlit deck nine feet off the ground. Sunshine kept away from the steps and stayed on the south end. If she wanted shade, she'd get under the table. The rest of the chickens respected her territory most of the time. But now and again, Mighty Mouse would hop contemplatively up the steps and wander, clucking quietly, to the far end where Sunshine stayed. Sunshine set up a rumpus whenever he did this and we would come running out, fearing the worst. We'd see then Mighty Mouse quietly pecking and murmuring some feet away from her as she squawked hysterically behind a chair. At first when he visited her, we feared he was mistreating her so we'd pick him up and drop him off the porch and he would fly down the nine feet with some grace, land neatly on his feet, crow with his adolescent call and strut, scratch and peck his way back to the flock. But we saw after the first few times that Mighty Mouse was acting the perfect gentleman. Gracious and gentle, he kept some feet away from her, pecked and chattered slowly about the porch. Sometimes he'd get up on the table and look in the window. He had, I think, some hope that he could tame Sunshine and have her as his own hen. When we saw all this, we watched him in action, allowed him to carry on his courtship if he could. He would wander about the porch approaching her and moving away, always gentle as she had her hysterics adamantly behind the chair. Then he would fly up to the railing, which put him twelve feet off the ground stretch his body up into a crow then fly heroically down to the ground below, but Sunshine never thought of him as anything but the enemy although he visited her many times, always gentle and polite.

Alice the raccoon got her in the end; I chased Alice away before she quite killed Sunshine, which left her blind and semi-comatose. I brought her in the house and she lived for days in that state. Once I put her out on the porch, hoping that the sun and her old territory might bring her back but she fell off the porch and landed, screaming and stuck in a cranny. Mighty Mouse and the white rooster got there before we did and we saw them then, the two roosters, squared off for a fight, neck feathers standing out straight in a ruff around lowered heads, beaks open and ready to clash, wings open and pointed down, rumps high to accentuate the curled tail-feathers. I broke it up quickly, took Sunshine back in the house. A day or two later, she finally died.

But since the white rooster could easily have killed Mighty Mouse, I gave the white rooster to a neighbor right away, and it was then that Mighty Mouse developed his full adult crow. He had fought now, or at least had squared off to fight, over his hen. So Mighty Mouse had the chicken yard to himself.

But Sunshine was dead now and what with Alice the coon and the neighbors' dogs, all the chickens died or were sold except for Mighty Mouse. For some time, he was alone without any other chickens and I had become disenchanted with chickens because they were so busy being killed by everyone, they seemed to have little time to lay eggs. And we enjoyed Mighty Mouse, bringing him in the house sometimes for children to pet and feed, putting him on the table after supper to clean up the crumbs and crow. But one day I went out to the barnyard and as I walked through the gate, Mighty Mouse walked toward me with a purposeful stride, looking into my face. It came to my mind that he needed hens, he needed a real life as a rooster. It seemed to be a powerful moment of communication between us, powerful but quick. I remember fighting briefly inside myself, not wanting the trouble of more chickens, wanting also the pleasure of his lonely need for society pulling him to us. But I felt that he was placing his life on the line. If he didn't get hens, he would die. It only took a few seconds to perceive and then decide. I stood, the gate still open in my hand, and I spoke aloud to him. "All right," I said, "I will get you hens." He turned then and strutted back and forth in front of me fluffing his feathers. I could see hope running through his body like lifeblood, reddening his comb, pulling his head high, sparkling his eyes. "Give me a week," I said.

The children patched the fence and Esta brought us Marlena and her two chicks. Mighty Mouse was gallant, not pushy. Marlena, her chicks being the main thing in her life at the time, paid little attention to Mighty Mouse. But he was full and happy now. He watched them, guarded them, showed them food, went with them about the yard. The chicks, Marly and Lena, grew up to be hens; Esta brought more hens: Pearl, Dokey, Hattie, half a dozen at any time. The fixing of the fence kept the dogs out and Alice, after killing Sunshine and seeing how upset I was about it, never returned.

Marlena was Mighty Mouse's queen, his partner, and his great love. He followed her, kept his eye on her, crowed in relation to her. She took her place as queen with thoughtful solemnity, helped him lead the other hens where the best food was, led them back to the chicken house when it rained. But the next summer, she took sick and for many days sat ruffled in the sun and Mighty Mouse sat by her day after day. When she finally died, he refused to leave the chicken house, wouldn't even crow in the morning, and we thought he'd die too.

For a couple of days, he sat on a shelf, his head crunched into his body his feathers askew. But Mighty Mouse, though small and lacking power, had endurance. On the third day of his mourning, I went into the chicken house and said to him sternly, "You have all these hens now; you must take care of them. You have responsibilities." Mighty Mouse glowered at me and then I stalked off into the house. In a few minutes, he emerged from the chicken house, crowed, and again took up his duties as a rooster.

The responsibilities of a rooster are many and no doubt I don't know them all. They crow to announce the day in the morning and they crow throughout the day to keep the hens in touch with the flock. They court and copulate with each hen every day to keep the eggs fertile. The courtship is done in this way: Mighty Mouse would approach a hen at an angle with the wing nearer to her, his wing feathers rattling, pointed to the ground, his feet rising high and thumping the ground rapidly as he turned away from her to show her his wing broadside. Then he'd approach her from the other side, dancing with the other wing down and rattling. If the hen put her head down, he could then climb on her back and mate with her. If she raised her head and ran a few steps forward, she was re-fusing him and he would try again later in the day. Many domestic roosters find it unbearable to go through all this courtship ritual daily with each hen, and simply jump un-ceremoniously onto the backs of their hens, very often causing bloody eggs and neurotic hens but Mighty Mouse went through the whole routine every time. If he found a supply of food he would call them to him. He watched over them, guarded them, led them to food. And in the evening, he called his flock home, counted them, and re-fused to go in the chicken house unless they were all in before him.

Across the next few years, Mighty Mouse's life was full and complex. One way or another, we kept about half a dozen hens in the yard. If a hen timed it right, I would allow her to set and raise chicks. Mighty Mouse was not very fertile and a couple of times Esta gave me fertile eggs from under her hens for my hens to raise.

Mighty Mouse had one sure daughter, striped like he was, and the tiniest chicken I've ever seen. We named her Speck. She was, nevertheless, a good layer, laying lots of tiny eggs for the two years that she lived. Since she wasn't tame like her father, I can say little about her life but that it was cheerful, sensible, and productive. Her death, however, was dramatic.

We knew the weasel lived under the house. She was a lesser weasel, weighing only a very few ounces, long, lithe, softly furred, dainty, with that tender innocence of expression only to be found in the most dangerous predators.

In early spring we found first an unfinished egg in a circle of striped feathers, then, some yards away, her headless body, one leg bone cleaned neatly of meat. The boys set traps all over the place, one of them baited with Speck's body but the weasel was too smart for us all and some weeks later paraded in broad daylight, as we were sitting on the porch, across the front yard. She was a lovely creature, light brown now, dancing along, inspecting everything with delighted curiosity, ducking into a ground squirrel hole and out again. She didn't, after all, get any more chickens and eventually moved away.

There was one time when Esta brought up a Cochin bantam rooster, a beautiful golden creature with feathered legs; and across the winter, the two roosters got along. But one evening in a snowy late winter, I found Mighty Mouse covered with blood from a broken spur, shivering and miserable. I brought him in the house, washed off the blood and warmed him in my arms until he stopped shivering. I didn't want to put him back out there until I could take the Cochin back to Esta, so I thought to let him roost on a kitchen chair and I went off to my bedroom but he followed me and stood rustling his feathers outside the door as I started to read. I brought him in then and he first sat in my lap then flew up to the top of the headboard and fell asleep. Somehow his sleep was contagious and, early as it was, I could no longer read, put down my book and slept like the proverbial log. Then at about five in the morning, he began his full-bodied resonant crowing. The sound crashed through my dreams, seemed to bounce and echo about the room like a lightning bolt. Knowing as I did that it would be repeated again and again for the next couple of hours or so, I staggered out of the bedroom, put the Cochin in a cage to take him back to Esta and got Mighty Mouse out of the house.

Mighty Mouse lived nine years. And during those years, he often found ways to contribute to our lives. I remember once a man stopped by who was not a friend and who would have liked to disrespect us. Not wishing to invite him into the house, I sat on the porch talking with him, leaving him on the road below, dueling with him in that quiet way folks have, disguised as an exchange of news. Mighty Mouse came to me with his questioning look. I took him onto my lap and when Mighty Mouse stood on my knee and crowed, the man had the sensitivity to acknowledge defeat and leave.

Often in the summer, we would gather with friends on the porch with a layout of food and drink and Mighty Mouse and one or two of the more intrepid hens would come to the porch, the shyer ones underneath on the ground, waiting for handouts. One summer we were plagued with flies and a flyswatter was installed on the porch. Mighty Mouse loved to eat flies more than any other food but they were beyond his abilities to catch. But that summer, he got his fill of flies as everyone swatted them and presented them to him. His enthusiasm spread to every gathering and that whole summer he seemed to bless us and our friends with the joy of life. He had the amazing ability to charm people who didn't care for animals. He would quietly join people with a style that was gentle, gracious and interested so that people again and again found themselves touched by his attention, then embarrassed to be so moved by a rooster. He just always had a certain courtly grace, and one couldn't help feeling honored at his attentions.

Toward the end, his legs bothered him. His spurs were so long, even the one that had broken off in the fight with the Cochin. He had to pick his feet up very high and raise them over the spurs for each step. There was some arthritis in his feet and legs too, so that it got to where he couldn't fly up to the roost but had to sleep on the floor of the chicken house. And he had stopped crowing. For weeks, he didn't crow. It was summer when it came to this point. One evening when I put the chickens away, I saw him looking, so dejected that I brought him into the house again. Even in summer here in the mountains, it's cold at night and that night it was raining; some of the water was seeping onto the chicken house floor where he was, and he couldn't get away from it. Again, I warmed him in my arms in the kitchen and he ate some seeds out of my hand. He knew he was dying, the hens knew it and showed it by their ruffled and wary stances, the few eggs they produced, their lack of enthusiasm about everything. They seemed to scorn him for his weakness and mourn his lack of presence. And Mighty Mouse knew it too.

There was no question now of saving his life, it couldn't be done. But for several days we kept him in the house where his legs could be warm and dry. He seemed to enjoy it when I would gently massage his feet. He sat on our laps, he followed us from room to room, limping painfully but still characteristically game and totally unafraid of us, liking our company. And we liked his. He particularly enjoyed mealtime, sat in my lap and I shared with him whatever I ate.

Within a couple days he was extraordinarily adept at snatching food from my fork before I brought it to my mouth. I remember my first shock at his enthusiasm for scrambled eggs. A young couple came to visit during that time and were totally charmed by him, petting him, feeding him, worrying over him. "He's too nice to die," they said. Since he was no longer crowing, he was no trouble in the house except for the droppings everywhere he went which I was glad to pick up. The feeling was that we were being honored greatly by his presence in the house, his charm and kindness to us in his last days, his grace in giving us this attention.

Then the rainy spell stopped and we went out on the porch to celebrate the sun. Mighty Mouse, of course, went with us. It was that same porch where Mighty Mouse had first courted Sunshine. It was one of those glorious days that happen when the sun comes out after rain, lush greenery, pure air, a faint haze of moisture rising through it, and the sun intensely welcome to everything. The birds singing passionately in the trees, rabbits and squirrels bustling everywhere, insects crawling, hopping, creeping and buzzing about. And in their wake, the hens scattered below us and across and down the road.

At first, Mighty Mouse responded to the sun, shaking his feathers, stretching his neck, walking back and forth on the sunlit deck, but the sound of clucking from underneath the porch called his attention to the two or three hens on the ground directly below us and he went to the edge of the porch and looked over, his head tilted to the side to see down the nine feet to where they were. For some long minutes he looked down, leaning further and further, his body crouched in yearning. Then he raised his shoulders, stretched out his wings and flapped down. I cringed at the thought of his crippled legs taking that landing, rushed to the rail to see but he was standing, standing tall. He started pecking the ground then and giving the staccato pecking call that says, "I've found food!" Our eyes teared up when we saw the hens come running, stretching their legs, their necks lengthened out, wings held up and flat, coming lickety-split from down the road and way across in the field to join him. Then there was such a clucking and scratching and bubbling and jostling of chickens down there on the ground beneath the porch that it seemed it must be radiating happiness for miles. After some minutes, wobbling on his bad legs, his head high, he crowed, not the full-bodied crow of his prime years, but the adolescent crow he had used at the beginning.

Naturally, I left him out with his chickens. And two days later, when I went to let them out in the morning, I found him dead in the chicken house.

MORE ROSY FINCHES

You know, these rosy finches are a lot more complex than that. Of course. Who isn't.

For one thing, there's an awful lot of individuality amongst them. Size, shape, coloring, movements, responses. There was one here this morning, a newcomer. Not a rosy feather on him. Nor brown either. Various shades of black and gray. Though an obvious grey-headed rosy finch somehow. For one thing, he was there on the wire spool with the rest of them. And his movements were right and everything. But he was being treated rather coldly, I thought. Always three or four inches of space around him, even if the others had to bump into each other to achieve it. And they didn't speak to him either. Surrounded by tails. He was nervous. He fidgeted on the edge of the wire spool for several seconds in the way they do to get the whole crowd to go — wiggling his back and stamping his feet. Actually, a couple of them looked

over at him in response to this movement but when he finally worked himself up into a high tension and took off,
the others had turned away so he just flew to the railing
and had a nice little drink of snow then came back. Looking embarrassed.

Later, another rosy finch was trying to get at what he
could, I suppose, smell through the shell of the sunflower
seeds. They really are stymied and fascinated by the sunflower seeds. It's just hilarious to watch their struggles
and frustrations over them. Perhaps I'm cruel to laugh at
this but if I don't, I'd squirm about it in unbearable sympathy.

The way the chickadees do it, they take a sunflower
seed, fly to the comparative privacy of a flattish, solid tree
branch, transfer the seed to their claws (talons? feet?), get
a good grip, then ax a hole in the husk or crack it, beating
on it very much like a woodpecker beats. On a clear day,
you can hear it for fifty yards.

But the rosy finches don't consider their feet. Or
maybe their necks are too long or — well, actually, they
just don't look the right shape to do that kind of work. So
they're always picking up sunflower seeds, mouthing
them for a while, then dropping them with a bewildered
look.

This morning, one rosy finch took a sunflower seed and gave it a real concentrated effort — it was beautiful. Like a silent comedy. He took it, mouthed it a bit among his peers on the wire spool, looking obliquely at the sky the while. Then flew to the railing, turning his back on the others, mouthed it and mouthed it, looking over his shoulder occasionally, turning this way and that. His embarrassment and his determination were splendid, but his lack of success a foregone conclusion. Then I moved my finger a quarter of an inch and the whole crowd crashed away. I couldn't see if he took his seed along or dropped it.

One thing I should say about their togetherness which rather changes my view of them. At times, there are just a couple here. Or one. Or three. And when they come like that, they act much more towards each other like chickadees do. One will be on the wire spool and one other will come. The first one will then run at the second quite fiercely. Then a third will perhaps arrive and the antagonism that the first rosy finch has to express makes it difficult for anyone to get a thing to eat. But, if then the whole flock comes, the situation suddenly changes, all arguments are forgotten and peace and the bubbling sweetness dominates the scene. Not a sign of animosity anywhere.

*Here begins the section of stories that might
be considered unpleasant. These are hard
stories to read. But I had to write them
because they show the realities of prey species.
If you want to think about a species as an
entity, or if you worry about the delicate
balance of nature — including natural acts,
or what we call "instinct," like loving, passion,
fighting, feeding the children — if you worry
about overpopulation of a species, like ours,
for instance; if your involvement with
animals goes beyond a delight in their beauty,
then read on. If not, there is much yet to read.
Skip to Coolie the Grackle and beyond!*

WILL RODENTS REIGN?

George Gamow used to say that after the next mass extinction, rodents would reign on earth. He was very impressed by the ways rodents have of adapting to practically any environment and the way they seem to enjoy life.

I've wondered a lot about the amazing creepy feeling that people, particularly women, have about mice and rats, spiders and snakes. They all claim that it's just a natural reaction, a first impulse. I know about first impulses as reactions, like stepping on the brake at need, skirting an obstacle while running, like typing, swimming, skiing, riding a bicycle; they are learned responses that become immediate, thoughtless. They become mindless impulses. People who jump onto a chair and scream in response to seeing a mouse are not deciding to do that, they are responding to very early training. That doesn't mean that their mothers showed them exactly that. It may have been that the mother felt the creepy response and tightened up, pulled back, gasped, put out the smell of fear, and then the little girl in her arms felt all that and went into a fit of nerves in response to what looked like nothing much on the surface. And after that, the little girl responded to the sight of a mouse in hysterical fear because she had been very frightened the first time in her mother's arms. This is the kind of emotional reaction that can go down through the generations. Somehow, I didn't pick up on that, loved animals, and found them to be interesting creatures, whoever they were. I was concerned while raising my children that they, particularly the girls who were older, had picked up some bad feelings about snakes from grade school and I wanted to be sure to put my ten cents into the argument. It happened that I was able to rescue a garden snake from a cat and take it home, and that evening, I had them sit in a circle and asked them to be calm and try not to scare the snake with any quick movements, showed them how to pet them front to back, not to disturb the scales. The boys were interested, the girls were tempted to jump back in a creepy giggly way but I told them there was nothing to be creeped about and in the end, they started to realize that this little garden snake was being slow and gentle and so should they.

SPARKLE AND THE MICE

It's undeniable. She was a beautiful creature. Irides-cent copper, well over four-and-a-half feet long, and fat, really quite fat, a rainbow boa. She liked to go about wrapped around Rarc's neck and then she'd reach her head toward my face and sniff me with her forked tongue and I could feel her breath on my cheek. Then, slowly and inexorably, she'd just wander across my shoulder, into the collar of my jacket, down my sleeve, and the thing to do was not to panic, but even if I didn't, it was hard to carry on a conversation or anything.

She was not my snake. I want to make that clear from the start. She was Rarc's. He had gotten involved with a bullsnake in the fifth grade and then that summer he saved up his money. What we did was pay the children for housework, and that year he was working for a penny a minute. That was in the early Seventies. After that, we had to give them raises, but that's what it was that year, and, working at a penny a minute, he saved up thirty-five dollars to buy Sparkle. He built a good big box, covered the bottom with dirt and some river rocks, and installed one of those mechanic's lights to keep her warm. Those tropical snakes have to stay at 80 degrees, which at least keeps her out of the kitchen and the beds and whatnot. If he'd got a bullsnake, I suppose it would have lived free in the house. We tended to do that sort of thing. Later we had a pigeon living on top of the refrigerator when he wasn't out with the chickens. And I'll never forget Luther, the guinea pig who used to live under the refrigerator. Anyway, Rarc got the boa and named her Sparkle.

It all started when we first moved to Lump Gulch. When the winter came on and there were so many mice, we finally decided that, even though they were innocent, we were being overrun and it was our house. So we got a regular ten-cent killer mousetrap and started killing them off. Then there were some that didn't die right away and we would listen to them scrabbling and crying and Stan would have to go and squash them with a waste basket and then it would pretty much haunt us for the rest of the day.

One morning, the trap wasn't there and we looked all around. A mouse had got just his foot caught in it and had hauled it behind the refrigerator. It was a really bad scene.

He was a gorgeous auburn color and he looked at us and his eyes said he was in deep trouble. He was the first mouse we took out to the fifth meadow and released. That's when I bought the catch-'em-alive trap and then we slept better.

As I say, you don't have to bait it, but we'd always put some seeds in there. The way it works is, first you wind it up. The mouse goes into the hole and steps on the plate in the middle of the passage. That sets off the mechanism and the whole wall sweeps across and knocks the mouse into a chamber with holes in it for air. And then the passageway is ready for the next mouse. I'll never forget the day we caught nine. We used to take them to the dump, turn them loose and watch them go off into the woods.

As far as I'm concerned, it's a better mousetrap. We'd put seeds in there and then the mice would be quiet and eat so we could sleep till morning. If there weren't seeds in there, they would scrabble at the holes all night to get out.

If they were all one tribe, they'd come out unhurt, but if they were strangers, that was another story. One time we forgot to put seeds in and we caught two and they had a fight. They're terrible fighters when they can't get away from each other. We found out about that the next morning when we took them to the dump, because the one had killed the other and eaten him. I suppose that would have been all right, more or less, but the horror of it was that the killer was now demented. He didn't just take a couple of bites because he was hungry, he gorged himself, leaving a few scraps of his erstwhile antagonist for us to shake out onto the snow. He was grossly fat, I never saw a wild creature nearly so fat as that, and he waddled out into the ditch without sense or direction. His eyes were crazy and his head rolled and he seemed to have no way of knowing where he was. It gave us the shivers just to look at him as he staggered away.

We have several kinds of mice around here. There's the regular city house-mouse, gray and kind of fierce looking, and there's the deer or white-footed mouse, a lovely creature, various possible shades of brown or tan or reddish with white underparts and white feet. The one we caught by the foot long ago was one of those. They're real wildlife, indigenous to the mountains here. They're the mice that coyotes and wolves eat a lot. Sometimes I've seen them in the meadows, leaping and dancing around. They can be gloriously happy and they have a terrific family sense, so that even if we forget to put the seeds in the trap, they wouldn't fight each other if they were family. Then there are the voles. That was a shock when we first caught a vole.

Voles look different, thicker and more compact with very short tails. And they move as if they were on wheels, smooth and quiet. We have shrews, too. I know because I had some apple cider jugs I was going to cut the bottoms off of to make cloches, but I hadn't done it yet and the apple cider jugs were out all winter under the snow and in the spring there were dead shrews, two or three of them, each in a different bottle, amazingly tiny with long noses. But they didn't come into the house.

Well, when Sparkle arrived, that all changed. I mean, she needed all the mice. Sparkle liked to curl up behind the rocks and, even though she was so big, sometimes she tied herself in such a compact knot that I had to look around in that little box to find her. She had a big bowl of water – held half a gallon – and she often went into the water. Rarc built up the dirt so she could slide up the dirt and into the bowl and she liked to go into the water and lie in it. Sometimes she'd lie in the water for days, sticking her head up once in an hour or so to breathe. That's the way reptiles are, they stay still for the longest time.

Then the question came into my head, what does it feel like to be a snake? Now, that's a tricky thing and many people these days say you shouldn't ask that kind of question. But I always think those questions you shouldn't ask are the important ones.

There was Sparkle curled up in her water, slowly reaching up with her nose every hour or so and breathing for a couple of minutes and then sinking her head down again under the water where the rest of her was curled up and staying there for days. The problem with understanding such a thing is that we're primates. And all primates are such nervous, chittery creatures, never satisfied, never at peace, always wanting to try something new. I feel it's a real shame that a species of that neurotic, unsatisfiable order of creatures should dominate the world, because we are always wanting something different and so we keep changing everything, even though everything usually goes along better without our changes. But what can you do when it's a primate you're talking to? Well, I didn't mean to go into this except to suggest the contrast between us and snakes, and Sparkle in particular.

She was clearly not waiting impatiently, or even patiently, for something to happen. I'd say she was enjoying a peace that we can't imagine, a quiescent, reptilian sensuality. Imagine what it would be like to be almost five feet long and fat at about four inches thick. Then imagine being that way and having no appendages and feeling not the slightest need for appendages. Then imagine having a small, flat, triangular head with jaws that can open several

times wider than your head is thick and that all that is normal and everybody else is either exotic or edible.

She never bit any of us except that when we first put her into the box, she bit Rarc. But that was just then and everything was new. Also, one time, Goldie caught her finger on Sparkle's tooth, but it wasn't Sparkle's fault at all. She had stopped eating, hadn't eaten for three months, so we asked Goldie, who had had snakes, what to do. She told about one snake she had, she had jammed a hot dog down it and then it got its appetite back. She even volunteered to try that with Sparkle because we were a little leery about doing it. So she came over and gently pushed a hot dog down Sparkle's throat and it got all the way out of sight but that was when Goldie caught her finger on Sparkle's tooth. And then out came the whole hot dog like toothpaste out of the tube. Goldie, not to be daunted, carved the hot dog to a point and stuck it in again and then used another hot dog to shove it in further. When she took the second hot dog out, the first one followed after and we all decided to quit. It wasn't more than a week or so later that Sparkle shed her skin and the mouse who had been living there with her in her box disappeared.

Then one day, I had to take the mousetrap to a friend who wanted to borrow it. I decided to set it, the night before I loaned it out, because Sparkle hadn't eaten for a week or so. Early the next morning there were two mice in there, young ones, and I took them to Sparkle's cage and put the trap in and slid off the top. The mice came eagerly out into Sparkle's world, pleased to be out of the constrictive trap. I could tell they were good friends. These were white-footed mice, dark brown on their backs, and they hadn't been fighting at all. They skipped into that place with open-eyed delight and encouraged each other and I could see they were lovely, lively individuals, gentle and happy. One ran up to Sparkle's water bowl and drank out of it and the other went to the seeds left over from the last mouse and they were very pleased and I loved them, they were sweet and innocent and I felt horrible and turned away. Sparkle had to have them, I told myself. She had to have live food. She wasn't mine. She mustn't starve. There were too many mice around here, eating our food and dirtying our pantry. No matter what I said, I didn't feel any better. All it served to do was to make me leave the mice there in the box.

Half an hour later, I went down and there was only one mouse. He had turned light tan in color and he was staring at Sparkle with one front foot pulled up to his chest and his mouth hanging open, trembling. Sometimes one has to be quick to keep from doing something painful. But if I had taken them out to the meadow or the dump while I had them in the trap, I'd have had to buy a rat or a hamster and feed Sparkle the rat or hamster. I guess if I was going to feel bad about the mice I shouldn't have had anything to do with it. Since the wolves and the coyotes have been cut back, and owls and hawks, too, and the dogs don't eat mice and we have hardly any cats, we're overrun with mice.

Other animals kill mice, what's the difference if I do? Why shouldn't I participate? I guess I had some neurotic guilt. The problem was, I liked them. Felt related to them. Then I felt guilty killing the one and torturing the other. Sparkle got him, too, later on, thank heaven. It's a real ethical problem, the ecological imbalances and all that, and the confusion which comes to the mind when you have a carnivore for a pet.

MOUSE AND HEREFORDS

Yesterday I went to take a mouse to the dump in the box trap we have. The quantity of mice we get out of the field would make our hearts and faces grim to kill them all, and their sweet paws, soft fur and thyroid eyes, twitching noses with whiskers. But the thing that got me the most was their individuality. That is, I can't know from one to the next what manners it will have, what coloring it will have, whether it will dash madly out of the box, walk with deliberate dignity, or have to be shaken forcibly out. Well, so I was driving to the dump, and right by the road were two Hereford bulls so I stopped to see them with the motor running and in gear. They were surely strange. They pawed the ground heavily so that I thought they were arranging beds to lie down on, then I realized that they hadn't a thought about lying down but that they were pawing the ground in some other sense. Also they kept scratching their horns and foreheads on the bank so that their curly foreheads were covered with dirt. The thing that got me the most was that with every breath they groaned actually vocally. I watched them for ten minutes or so, finally daring to put the car out of gear, and they continued doing all these things. I couldn't think of any explanation for any of it except that they seemed to have bugs in their bonnets about their masculinity, that they were sex maniacs yearning for a lay. It seemed that they were really quite uncomfortable and I would have thought that they would soon die of such discomfort except that sex is such a vital urge that the promise of it is the central goal of adult life.

I took the mouse then, and as soon as I opened the box, his whiskers were out and soon he courageously followed them under the car. I gunned the motor and saw him running like hell away to hide in some kinnikinnick twenty feet away. Hours later when we went to the movie, the two bulls were still there pawing and groaning but when we came back from the movie, there was a change, that is, there was a score more or less of cattle around them which we had difficulty in passing. I wasn't able to see if the bulls were still pawing and groaning. I think not.

THE CAPTAIN OF THE MICE

I have always had a problem with mice and the problem is that I'm really quite sympathetic to them and see them as reasonable creatures living sweet domestic lives. They are loving, family-oriented little creatures who love to explore and love to store away food in special places. For a very long time the mice multiplied in the cabin until they were keeping me awake at night scuttling about among my books, moving sunflower seeds and dog food from one place to another, storing them behind the books or in my shoes. I was always hesitant to put my foot into a boot without shaking the boot out first. I had learned this precaution in the desert but then it was in case a scorpion had taken up residence. In the Rockies, it was an expectation to find dog food or sunflower seeds stored there by mice.

One day I came home late, exhausted after a hard hike through a blizzard. I arrived after dark and I was so cold and tired that I didn't bother to build a fire; I just got into bed and piled a lot of blankets on and fell asleep. I must not have moved all night long because in the morning I felt a little tickle on my back and found that a mouse had built her nest against my back, the only warm spot in the place. Thank heavens I woke before she had her babies in it.

There are those have-a-heart traps and we had used them in Lump Gulch, filled them with mice and then driven them to the dump down the road. But here, I was afoot and the distance a mouse will travel to get back home can be measured in multiple miles. I felt there was no choice. I was losing sleep with all the racket at night. There was one final occasion when a nest full of mice emerged from behind my mattress and one after the other they all ran across my recumbent body until finally I grabbed the backscratcher and commenced whacking at the last one, hitting it, killing it, crying out while I was killing it, "Oh! You poor little darling!"

When the population of mice increased in my two-room cabin to where there were always nests around my bed, I felt it was time to kill them. It seemed to me that it had come to the point that I had either to move out or to kill mice. The other possibility did occur to me, but I gave it short shrift: I could become their servant, spend my days and nights studying them and serving them, but I rejected that. I had my own things to do. Obsession has never been my trump suit. Like the flies in the kitchen at Lump Gulch, whom I had paid attention to and could follow their emotions and their schemes, it had come to the point of "either them or me." Their little feet running across my body woke me if their squeaking and scuttling hadn't already, and it was hard for me to get back to sleep, what with watching them show each other routes up the bookshelves to hide piles of food behind the books or the excrement they left wherever they went.

Thus began the long slow and agonizing mayhem. I bought traps, set them and at some time in the night I'd hear a snap and the frantic rustling of the mouse whom I hoped was dying quickly. There were awful occasions when I'd have to get up and drown a mouse in a container of water, then try hopelessly to get back to sleep. If I did, or if I had miraculously slept through the killing, I was faced in the morning with the question: should I take out the corpses before breakfast or after breakfast?

There was one mouse very early on who caught his foot in the trap, bounced down the stairs, me in distress for his pain as I tried to catch him and drown him but he escaped, managed to tear his foot out of the trap, and slid out the door and under the house. This moment while writing this sad tale is the first time I realize that it was this mouse that was undoubtedly the lame mouse who was the Captain of the mice during that whole ghoulish period while I was killing off the mice, one by one. He had a syncopated shuffle that I could hear going across the floor. He held his head higher than the other mice and I could often see the shadow of his ears going jerkily across the books in the bookcase by moonlight.

One after the other, I killed those mice, beautiful little auburn-coated deer mice, and I would toss their bodies out on the edge of the terrace and someone, probably the

ermine, would get them within twelve hours. Then there were fewer and fewer mice in the house and I felt I could almost clean house now with some effect. Then there was but that one mouse left; the lame mouse still paced the floor, his round ear shadows huge on my books. I knew that he knew that the baited trap held his death if he cared to go that way.

Mice are not made to be hermits. One night, the trap snapped once more, and it was he: this time he did a good job of it and put his head in the center and sprung the lever. In the morning, I looked at his corpse, expecting a giant or a great deal of frontal lobe development but there was nothing – he looked just like a dead mouse. I didn't even detect a flawed foot, maybe a slightly bent leg bone. I tossed his body in the usual place over the terrace and within a couple of hours he was gone. And for a while, there were no more mice in the house. At last I could clean the counter, the dishes, pots and pans, with a sense of achievement.

I thought about him a lot. What had he thought of me? Was he right to think that? One has to forgive cats for killing mice because that's what they are structured to do. Am I structured to kill mice also? To some extent, it must be so. Mice, like rabbits, flies, deer, sardines, and un-doubtedly ourselves also, are prey species, and are geared to lose population to the predator just enough to maintain a good well-balanced ecology. I guess this is not the place to discuss the overpopulation of our species. I think I will strive to forgive myself for killing that mouse. But I will not deny the beauty and passion of his life.

SMALL ANIMALS

The parakeets live in our back room and fly all day among the rafters and go to their cage in the evening where I lock them in and cover them. There are three of them. Baby Doe, the turquoise female, suddenly one day didn't have her tail feathers or the feathers of one wing and therefore couldn't fly at all. We kept her in a cage for a day but she and the others were so disturbed by that that we started letting her out a couple times a day to hop around on the floor. But I was troubled about it because I couldn't find the feathers. Such pretty feathers they have and I like to save them but they simply weren't there which was impossible since she hadn't left the room, so I kept going in there to look.

Baby Doe had been hopping around for awhile and I went in to put her back in the cage. I found her a few feet from the pump room, a little closet that holds the water tanks and, because of the need for access to certain pipes,

196

is open to the narrow space under the floor. As I stooped over to pick her up I saw a flash of white movement by the pump room. I rose to look over and saw a sweet and dainty pure white face looking, it seemed, questioningly at me. I simply stood and gaped. At which she seemed to think her question answered and scooted toward Baby Doe a long and agile white body looking like what a dachshund should be but never is. Realizing finally that I must act or watch my parakeet be gracefully killed, I waved my hands and, I'm embarrassed to say, gobbled much like a turkey. The beautiful creature then looked up at me brightly, turned, and vanished under the floor.

We sealed off the pump room within the hour. In a month or two Baby Doe could fly again. It was spring. But I had seen the weasel.

In the spring, on the porch, I saw the weasel again. This time she was light brown. She came dancing out from under the house and skipped along the edge of the porch poking her nose into everything along the way, a bit of pipe, a bucket of water, a tipped-over box, then a ground squirrel hole and I held my breath until she came out again.

Evidently no one was at home. Less than a week later she killed Speck, our smallest hen, a very small ban-tamweight hen but a good egg layer. We found a pile of feathers with an unfinished egg in the middle and then Speck's body some yards away; with one leg daintily removed and the head missing. We set several traps then but the weasel avoided them and we didn't encounter her again until the rabbits had been here for a while.

It was the middle of September when a neighbor called me and asked if I'd like a few rabbits, either in the freezer or in the back yard, my choice. "Oh, the yard, of course," I said. I could put them out there with the goats and the geese and the chickens. It would be lovely, and they'd clean up the spilled seed. We turned them all loose in the hay shed, which seemed a good place for them to nest, and also they could eat the hay.

There were three boxes of rabbits. We took them out and opened them one by one. The first box contained one rabbit, a female Cheshire, white, with blue-black around her eyes and ears. The second box contained two beautiful rabbits, one rusty brown and the other blue-gray, both with an indescribable sheen on their fur. These were two satin rabbits, both males. In the third box there were three brothers, satin mixed with something else, one gray runt and the other two speckled with a white base.

At the time, I remember feeling a little irritated that she had given me such an imbalance of the sexes. They should be paired or perhaps there should be five does and one buck, if that's how they mate. But there it was, five males and one female. I decided to not look the gift horse in the mouth. As it turned out, I learned so much from them the way they were, I can't imagine now anything better for learning.

Then we loaded up the hay shed with the third cutting of hay, one hundred bales of it and piled it up in the hay shed. There was a difficulty about it this year because the rabbits were everywhere in there. This was when we'd had the rabbits about a week and they had stayed in the garden. There were two openings out of the garden. Even humans could see them plain as day not to mention the three other invisible holes I found out about later. But these rabbits had been born in boxes and lived always in boxes and the garden seemed for a while to be the nicest box imaginable and they danced about in it with the sunlight shining down and eating the hay, running about and sniffing out all the places and what was there. The thing they'd do that endeared me so much was they'd find some new marvel and they'd sniff it and then they'd jump straight up into the air and I couldn't figure out any explanation for it at the time except the phrase "jump for joy."

When the little blind bunnies in the nest are approached and disturbed they jump and the nest turns suddenly from a feather-soft tender bundle into something like a fast-cooking pot of popcorn as each blind bunny jumps and jumps again. This serves two purposes, I think. First, it is quite disconcerting to any passing critter like me for instance and one would tend not to step on such a thing, even to think twice before trying to take one of these jacks-in-the-box as a bite to eat or sniff them over to see which is the choicest morsel. One tends rather to be taken aback. The other purpose is, I believe, to stimulate the milk flow of the mother rabbit. Since this is the characteristic movement of healthy bunnies in the nest, she is assured that they're full of pep and ready for a bit of sup.

The question of what purpose is served by an action is one thing and another thing entirely is what stimulus causes that action to be made and yet another is what feelings are washing across the individual doing it. All these things need to be understood if one is to understand, for instance, rabbits.

Words are so important when you're trying to think. If the language and the culture give us words like "instinct" and "anthropomorphism," anyone tends to try to understand the word and then fit their observations into it. In the study of animal behavior, these words as a way of looking at an animal gives you nowhere to go, nothing to think, no way to understand the animal.

Other species besides ourselves don't use words to think with. This doesn't mean they don't think. They think with their senses; they think with their bodies, and with their body chemistry. They think with their own memories and with the memories of their species. Some folks are born wise. Rabbits are born to hop, but that's not all that they're born with. They're born with a lot of things that we're born with, too.

The fact is that people are more interested in feelings than anything. I am not immune from this interest myself. Therefore when I saw these rabbits jump in this way, I warmed to them because it seemed they were showing their feelings to me and that that jump seemed something generally translatable to "Whoopee!" or perhaps "Hallelujah!" Or it might be that it was some discovery that they made in that moment, a smell perhaps which may have either thrilled them in itself or directed them to a realization which startled them. In which case I could translate it to "Wow!" or perhaps "Yikes!" The fact remains that by the time they'd become more or less mature, that is, by about Christmas, I no longer saw this charming expression from them and assume that their youthful high spirits were muted by the heaviness of a more mature attitude.

At first the rabbits stayed in the garden and I could see their hierarchy building as the days and weeks went by. From the very beginning I brought them cabbage twice every day not because they needed it but so that I could always get close to them. The ritual was an important time in the day.

The first day I squatted down with my cabbage and held it out. I could see them all but wondered if they would come to me. But the doe came over and as she ate cabbage from my hand, I looked around at the others and saw how they watched the proceedings with their backs turned and seeming to be looking at something else. Scratching then licking the foot they scratched with, nibbling on something then stopping in mid-nibble in fascination with the goings-on between me and the doe. The runt, on the other hand, stood a few feet away and watched with what seemed an intelligent and thoughtful look on his face then after a bit came closer and I stretched out my other hand and gave him a piece of cabbage. "That one," I thought, "is my favorite. His name is Silky." I scattered the rest of my cabbage around more or less in the direction of the shyer rabbits and went my way.

As I said before, the rabbits stayed there, all of them, for some weeks. But the garden became less and less a peaceable kingdom as they matured. Of the two satin rabbits the blue-black one which I named Blue became the closest friend of the doe. They seemed to be usually together and where she led he followed. Not that he was a wimp at all, quite the contrary. He was developing into a sleek and powerful animal and I believe achieved his position near her from his power. Though whenever I was out there, he seemed docile enough. It was his brother, whom I named Satin, who rose up as the ferocious monster and chased the others about. Satin was without doubt the most beautiful of the rabbits but his position was as the bully and more and more as time went on I saw him chasing Silky and his spotted brothers.

One of Silky's brothers, the black-spotted one, the neighbor had named Horny because of his early propensity to hump everything he could get up on from the time he crawled out of the nest. It was he that I finally felt a compunction to rescue from what must have been Satin's bullying when I found him hiding day after day not daring to come away from this tiny niche he had in the hay even to eat the cabbage I gave him nor to look anywhere but straight in front of him. So after several days of this I took him and put him over the fence into the goat yard.

And two days later I did the same for Silky. When I came out with cabbage and Satin grabbed Silky by the behind in his teeth and Silky was screaming and tugging for an eternity of seconds, I threw a rock at Satin but missed and the next day I put Silky with Horny and had two rabbits in the goat yard.

By this time the hay had become a most attractive maze of hallways and rooms. I had taken Horny out of one dismal room but left his and Silky's brown-spotted brother in another nicer corner where he seemed to have created a quiet though timorous life eating alfalfa and watching the doe from a distance. I called him Conservative.

For several days Horny and Silky enjoyed this new space. They were, in fact, ecstatic and I saw them sometimes leaping high in the air with their heads thrown back or running in circles. The alfalfa, however, in the goat yard did tend to be guarded by goats. Also the ground was hard and packed and I wondered where they were going to spend the nights when the winter got on.

I was also expecting at least these two to mate with wild does and I watched eagerly as the wild rabbits watched me feeding Silky and Horny and, as the weeks passed, the wild rabbits got closer and closer until, from keeping always ten yards or so away, they would still be there as I slowly approached as close as two or three yards. But if I tried to toss cabbage pieces to them they'd run away. The fact was that Silky and Horny never were seen consorting with the wild rabbits and I really don't think they bred with them because the wild rabbits look as pure as ever. By this time even Silky and Horny were twice the size of the wild ones and still growing, looking as though they'd win in a tug-of-war but lose in a race.

And so for a couple of weeks everything was delightful and every rabbit I saw was happy as could be but then one day everything happened at once. First of all I took cabbage out there and as I climbed over the fence there were Silky and Horny below me standing as usual on their hind feet, noses wiggling and forefeet dangling in the posture people try to teach their dogs to get into and call it "beg" or "sit up." On rabbits, I think I'd call it "eager." They got their cabbage and I went to look in the garden at the others and there was blood on the snow and pale blood on the doe's back. I counted the rabbits. There were Blue and Satin and Conservative, all well. I looked again at the doe. She did seem to be quite a bit slimmer than before. It was at that moment that I began calling her "Mother" though I still wasn't in the least sure what had happened.

That afternoon Satin came out of the garden and into the goat yard and began attacking Silky. I saw them out the window racing in circles. Then Silky would make an amazing running leap rising three or four feet into the air

and Satin would aim and leap at him in the air and sometimes manage to bite him in the side as they were high in
the air. The picture of them thus has remained in my
memory. Satin powerful and gleaming, ears flattened,
hind legs almost straight behind him, leaping through the
air, rabbit-turned-bullet, and Silky arched, curving sideways to dodge this missile, delicate and sensitive, his intelligent face turned to see his antagonist's teeth almost
closing on his flesh, but in the air Silky twisted and pulled
himself away from the teeth so that when the two of them
landed they were apart and the chase could go on.

And so it did go on for the rest of that day and the
next, I in an agony in the kitchen watching this admit-
tedly beautiful and spectacular sight going on and on. A
neighbor offered to shoot Satin but I declined, my reason
being only that it would upset my pregnant goats.

Strangely these mornings Satin would sit very close to
me while I milked the goat and on the third morning I
caught him and put him in a box and drove him half a
mile to a meadow with a willow grove where I dumped
him out.

The road slopes down between the willows and the
meadow to a turn-around. I stopped close to the top of
this slope and took Satin out of his box on the willow side
of the road. He very much wanted to stay in his box. I put

down a little pile of sunflower seeds for him and drove to the turn-around. As I started back up, he ran toward the road, his ears forward as if the sound of the car were the sound of my arrival in the yard with a handful of cabbage. Then as the engine roared to pull the car up the incline he stopped at the edge of the road and crouched there with his ears laid back seeming with his posture to be begging to be either picked up or run over. I roared past him and that was that. I look for him still at that patch of willows but I've never seen him again. I told my neighbor about it. She said, "Coyote-food." I'm more inclined to think "dog-toy." Anyway, that's what I did and I have to live with it.

So very often, trying to help one person causes devastation to another. I don't know what to do about that but pick favorites and then work on justifying that.

Bleakly, I watched Silky as he tried to move into Satin's place as the bully. It was a foolish move on his part, he being small and weak and after several days of his chasing Conservative around the yard, he got badly beat up and began to come to me for cabbages surreptitiously with a ragged ear and not placing his weight on his right forefoot.

It was about now that Mother brought out her bunnies into the November sunshine and I remember sitting out there on the snow, cabbage in one pocket and sunflower seeds in the other, trying to tame them. It was an impossible task as they'd been deep under the hay for nearly a month and had half-a-dozen routes back in to their nest. But I got to watch them study and explore the world as they saw it enlarging or throw themselves on their backs to nurse from Mother's low-slung belly. There were six of them, one wild-colored but with a white blaze, one black with a white collar, one albino and three white with black spots and I went out every day to see them but one day they didn't come out and there was blood on the snow and somewhere around that time Mother was bloody again and I thought she'd had another batch but I never saw the second batch or ever the first batch again because the weasel had arrived.

Silky's health got worse and I saw to my horror his right shoulder swelling up and the right forefoot not in use day after day until finally I thought he'd die so I went out with a strong mixture of terramycin in water and some cabbage and dipped out as much terramycin as I could on the cabbage leaves which was quite a bit and Silky enjoyed the medication tremendously and seemed to feel better after that, though the bump was still there. A few days later as I was milking the goat I felt him placing his paws on my back which was an unprecedented bit of intimacy so that, although I never stop milking in the

middle unless it's a very urgent matter, I stopped and saw
that the bump had not been a bone problem but an
abscess and had broken open exposing the sinew of his
side like Rembrandt's Anatomy Lesson. As I always have
an antiseptic within reach of the stanchion, I placed a pile
of sunflower seeds in front of him, then dabbed into the
abscess with the antiseptic hoping the first dab would do
it all because that stuff can sting. But he went on keeping
still and eating the seeds until I'd done a good job of it and
then came back every day for several days for another
treatment, then showed it to me when, for instance, the
scab cracked and later when it fell off. The thing healed
up splendidly and he recovered the use of his foreleg as
soon as the abscess popped, but he never got over the un-
kempt look or regained any social status.

Conservative grew and grew and although he always
remained cautious and never was fast, his very weight
gained him a respect. I suspected him of having given
Silky his abscess so my heart never went out to him but I
fed him along with the rest. By the first of the year, Silky
and Horny were left alone by Conservative if they were
outside the whole palisade, though at times I'd see them
in with the goats, never in the garden except one time
which I will tell about. Mother still stayed entirely in the
garden and Blue, her chosen consort, stayed most of the

time with her. Conservative had the run of every area and was conscientious in his efforts at patrolling them all. Horny seemed to have expended all his sexuality before puberty and now never was near Mother or any rabbit except Silky. The one time I saw Silky in the garden was when Mother was all over blood again from having another litter and, Nature being the tyrant she is, was very much in heat so that although she was extremely busy smoothing out a patch of dirt behind the hay shed, the males, all except Horny, were mad with sexual desire for her and I watched as Silky waited trembling while first Blue then Conservative mounted her, bloody as she was, she ignoring them as she worked on this patch of ground, then after they both went away Silky slipped through a hole in the fence and humped her passionately as she continued in her work. I looked at the patch of ground the next day and could see no achievement or meaning to it. Perhaps it only served to keep her still so they could impregnate her again.

Horny was a strange little fellow. He wasn't much bigger than Silky. Their brother Conservative must have weighed about what the two of them together did. Horny avoided trouble. Whenever anyone was chasing someone, Horny was elsewhere. During the great sex orgies between Mother's pregnancies, Horny was busy eating or exploring. Wherever some great drama was, Horny wasn't.

So that when, in February, Horny showed up with his belly and all four of his paws bloody, I was amazed. He didn't let me catch him and I was unable to medicate him at all. In a couple days he seemed cheerful enough although blood was still there in spots. I don't know if it was Horny's wound or the birth of the next litter that marked for me the beginning of the end, which seemed to be only a number of tragic incidents which all happened to happen at once, or at least all within a month or so, so that by the first of May the rabbits were all dead or, in the case of Mother, locked up. I can give you the chronology of what I know but it's not enough to really piece together any certainty of anything. All I can say has essentially been said, that is, that rabbits do live sensitive, passionate, highly individual and serious lives.

And so here is what little I know of their deaths.

Shortly after the startling display of Horny's bloody belly, I saw Mother outside not only of the garden but of the whole palisade. She seemed obviously to be looking for a new nesting place and I hoped with little hope that she'd find one that the weasel would not find. With her, guarding her like the queen's own personal bodyguard, was Blue.

Two nights after that we heard a shriek in the dark and ran out turning on the porch light and saw a big German shepherd dog and the next morning Blue without the loss of a drop of blood was clearly dying. He was comatose and had pressed himself into a cranny where I could watch him through the window. I assumed internal hemorrhage and thought of mercy killing but knew for sure the harm that doing it would do to me and so refrained, built rather a cave around him of loose bricks with food and water and shelter. It took him two days but finally he died and we buried him in the garden. Mother went then to the car we use as a goat barn and had her litter in the trunk. We found them there, a large fluffy wad of fur covering naked squirming blind infants. We fixed up a hutch and took the bunnies by handfuls and put them in a padded box in the hutch, caught Mother and put her in, hoping she wouldn't eat them as several friends and neighbors predicted she would.

There were nine of them, one totally wild-colored, one black with a white collar, one gray and the others variously white with brown or blackish spots, seven of them females. We touched them every day at least once and thus tamed them. Mother is a mellow doe and understanding and in spite of her long history of lost litters, she raised these bunnies with assurance.

Within a few days after the removal of Mother and the litter to the hutch, both Silky and Horny disappeared, Silky first and then Horny two or three days later. There are two likely explanations of this. One is the German shepherd that got Blue. And the other is that the weasel, thwarted of her monthly feast of infant rabbit, took the weakest rabbits she could get and ate them instead.

This left us with only Conservative running loose and he spent most of his time under Mother's hutch. When the nine bunnies were a month old, Mother built a new nest in a corner of the old nest and gave birth to six more bunnies. We quickly took away the older litter but not until one of the new bunnies had died, a gray one, maybe trampled by the older bunnies.

Conservative stayed under the hutch until one day he moved down by the basement door and acted strangely and later he was shaking violently and chattering his teeth in the rain and he turned away from the cabbage and I thought, "Let him die in peace," though I hadn't known till then that he was even sick. The rain turned to snow and a couple hours later I went out and he was dead and stiff at the bottom of the stoop to the back door and I picked him up on a shovel for fear of his disease and buried him in the mine hole out back and when I returned at the bottom of the stoop was his shape left in the snow.

I worried a great deal about Conservative's disease and watched Mother and her two broods as well as worrying about the wild rabbits catching it.

For about a week after his death I didn't see any, but then I did know there are quite a few of them and two still watch me from one or two yards away. The other day I saw two chasing each other all around the house and I knew there would be a litter growing in a den nearby and for a moment I warmed, but then I knew also that the weasel would get them, and for an instant I remembered the weasel's beauty, then washed the admiration of it away with the memory of Speck's body, her unfinished egg framed in torn-out feathers. But then seeing the rabbits chasing each other, I realized they must both be bucks and fighting over a doe which meant that there were three or possibly four where there should most comfortably be two and a litter of half-dozen or so, each rabbit an interesting individual.

And each weasel, of course, likewise.

And so from six young rabbits in the fall through much pain and loss we now have fifteen rabbits in the spring and more to come. The pain and loss cannot be denied nor can the increase in numbers nor the fact that all the survivors are in hutches. Multiplying it out and finding that if they all lived, say six bunnies every month and ready as rabbits are to breed at age three months, that starting in early October, by the Fourth of July, with ideal conditions and no deaths at all, we should have approximately six hundred rabbits in the garden. I found myself finally saying to myself, "How fortunate that I had only one doe or we'd be up to our ears in weasels."

CRITTER SUICIDES

There were two incidences of suicide in which I found the perpetrator expected me to help.

The first was a tufted-eared black Abert's squirrel, an endangered species who could live only at an elevation of about seven to eight thousand feet with an open forest of trees predominately Engelmann spruce and Ponderosa pine.

Funny thing about endangered species, they very often seem to all get in danger of erratic behavior, depression, a loss of interest in life. People in the mountains had noticed how many Abert's squirrels seemed lethargic or nuttier than a squirrel should be and also seemed to run without looking at traffic out across the road. You could tell their little smashed corpses from other squirrels, ground squirrels or chipmunks because the Abert's squirrels were deep black.

So I was driving down Boulder Canyon, came around a bend and there, where I had often seen Abert's squirrels, was an Abert's, uncharacteristically checking my speed and I could see he was planning to have me run over him.

I slowed, watched his disappointment turn to anger. I stopped the car, rolled down the window and shouted out, "Not on me you don't commit suicide. You'll have to find someone else!"

He stood at the side of the road and watched me in disgust as I slowly increased speed and went on down the canyon to Boulder.

On the way back home, I looked at the pavement at that place and there he was, a black pancake on the road; just where he had asked me to do it someone else had done it. Most probably they didn't even notice.

The second such occasion was a little dog at a farmhouse beside a highway somewhere mid-country, a little dog with a very expressive face.

The traffic was tight. I was unable to stop. I saw this little face with a huge anguish and horror for life as it had become in his home. Love and idealism had shattered. Something terrible had happened in that farmhouse that he found totally unbearable and he had determined to get himself run over. He was frantic to get run over. All this I could see in his face as he peered out from the bushes into the traffic.

This next part may be hard for you to believe, I suppose, if you haven't already fallen off a long time ago. I have found, and I believe it happens to everyone, that faces communicate and telepathy is not only a common occurrence but, in fact, it's constant.

The little dog chose my car perhaps because he detected my admitted excess of sympathy. There was naturally no time for me to soothe him, tell him that hard times pass. I could only telepath to him:

"Not the front wheel; I would swerve and I would also suffer with guilt forever. If you jump between the front and the back wheels, I won't feel to blame."

So, obedient dog to the end, that's what he did and I felt one bump as my back wheel only went over him and the traffic carried me away while undoubtedly also car after car finished the job very quickly behind me.

The question arises, "Why write about running over a dog? Why not just tell us meaningful stories of hope and love, of people doing great things?"

But you see, those things were there in that instant. In that instant, that dog and I let our hair down and had a discussion about a dog's possibilities in life. He was not a dog who could wander off and look for a better situation.

Most dogs hurl themselves into the life that comes to them, as do most humans, not looking around for a fit, so potentials very seldom have a chance to fulfill themselves.

Those finches in the Galápagos Islands – small beaks for small seeds in wet years; big beaks for breaking big seeds in dry years, the two kinds of beaks to be found in the same nest. Studies have been made. When the year will be dry, a preponderance of big-beaked finches hatch; when it will be wet, there are many more of the small-beaked birds. The ones unfitted to the year perform the very important function of keeping the possibility of the other climate prepared-for. They're there because the potential for them must go on existing for the continuation of the species.

That's a bit rough on those unfit representatives, rough also for a very sensitive little dog to be caught up in an environment that requires self-assured independence.

An interesting thing has happened in the thirty years since I had that encounter with that Abert's squirrel. In spite of bark beetles and land-clearing for roads and houses, the Abert's squirrel is having a comeback. Somehow, the species softened its strictures about altitude. Maybe even it decided that lodgepole pine was okay. Perhaps it was an early response to global warming or perhaps a mutation. In any case, the Abert's squirrels have tremendously widened their altitude requirements and I've seen them even as far up as nine thousand feet and I've heard of sightings of them down to near six thousand feet. In spite of their increased population, they're not getting run over near as much as they were thirty years ago. Evidently, they got past their depression and are now feeling hope.

KNOWING THINGS

Somebody told us lately that schizophrenics always know what mood people are in. This made me suspect that I must have a certain amount of schizophrenia in my makeup, because I seem to read feelings more than other folks do. I'm encouraged also because this guy says that if someone with schizophrenia tells you what mood you're in, whether you agree with him or not, you may be sure that he's right!

So many people these days say that if you suggest that anybody except humans has a feeling, you're being anthropomorphic, a stupid and dirty word. I agree, though, that the Walt Disney approach to nature, the assumption of innocence and adorableness is nothing more than a really heavy wall anyone can put up to protect themselves from understanding what's going on. Very often, it's the first thought, though. I believe that I was guilty of calling the rosy finches "innocent" a couple months ago, as I was overwhelmed with their beauty. I can think of no excuse for this. My only hope is that I will be one who "tears off the veil; tears the temptation, the mist the heart wears, from its eyes" and perceive the fullness of the lives around me.

Stan showed in one of his films the fierce and savage violence in the cry of an infant. There's no need to be blinded by maternal instinct. Maternal instinct is a magnificent thing, a marvel of life, but I needn't use it to hide behind. Best I use it to maintain interest, to enrich what clarity I can find in my perceptions with love and understanding. I told Betsey the other day, I aspire to know everything and love it. I remember once praying that I wanted to know everything. Now, maybe a dozen years later, I've the same prayer with this amendment, that I'll love it. Some change shown here. I'm not pleased with bitterness. I think bitterness is the other side of the coin of cuteness. Just another evasive tactic.

COOLIE THE GRACKLE

The grackle died, as he had lived, with perfect timing in relation to my life and needs. It was what they call uncanny. He had been the bandage, actually a solid thread of joy, across those last two years of fairly constant misery.

The grackle was a little bird that I raised from the time he fell out of the nest at the age of just a few days. He was by far the smartest, quickest-learning creature I have had the honor to care for. He came like an angel to see me through the death of Tree, the great goat, who was the best friend I ever had, then through the divorce and then, about when I had found homes for all the animals and put the house up for sale, he died. Two years. A wonderful lovely soul. His name was Coolie.

A grackle is a small blackbird of a species to which no one to my knowledge has paid much attention. They don't seem even to have acquired a name for their grouping, like "a wedge of swans" or a "murder of crows." If that is so, I'll give them one: "A clan of grackles," as it seemed to me with Coolie and later watching others, that they were clannish, with ties like blood ties. Grackles run together like coyotes do and eat everything, animal or vegetable, that they can snatch up into their beaks. Their first preference is insects. I have seen them dodging waves while hunting on the Pacific coast, daintily picking grass seeds in the Rocky Mountains, scrounging garbage in small-town streets from coast to coast, following cows and tractors for tossed-up bugs. In that way, they are the coyotes of the Kingdom of the Birds. They have all the intelligence and the adaptability that coyotes have and more. They are highly social. Like goats, they love mischief more even than food.

When Coolie arrived in my life, I was a respected member of society, had worked with a great deal of devotion to my husband and his work for nearly thirty years, raised five children, handled the business, had a delightful house and a back yard full of animals. I was involved deeply in the place where we lived, and had lived for twenty-three of those thirty years. I could tell you where the wild strawberries would probably be ripe this week, where and when to pick red clover; I knew the magic places and the special trees, knew how to get to where the various edible mushrooms could be found in a good year, knew what weather would come by how the clouds looked as they came over the Divide, all those very local, very specific knowledges that anyone gains who walks about a lot in one area. I had chickens and geese laying eggs, a greenhouse producing salads; I had dogs, cats, ducks, half-wild rabbits and most especially there were the goats, the registered dairy goats peaking at above a gallon of milk a day each, which plethora I had learned to make into various fabulous cheeses and had some of these cheeses aging in the cellar at all times. These goats delighted me with their warmth and intelligence and love of life always and I never wearied of their company. The great goat, Tree, I had raised in my lap with a bottle and she was, when Coolie arrived, at the age of eighteen, queen of the barnyard, emanating wild animistic wisdom and she and I loved each other inordinately.

My husband and I had had five children who were now grown, mostly lived amiably nearby and were beginning to have children of their own. I was writing stories and books and what I wrote was being published and read by people whom I greatly admired.

By the time the grackle died two years later, Tree had died, the dogs had died, my husband had left me, the goats were sold, the rest of the animals had found various homes, the house echoed without its books and artworks and was now the worst place on the planet for me to live.

When the grackle died, my empire of thirty years making was crumbled to a rotting encumbrance; I was part of the discarded rubble; my position of honor a tragic farce; and I was fifty years old.

When Coolie arrived, already named by my three-year-old granddaughter Iona, he sat mostly on the edge of a basket in the kitchen, a small gray blob with intense eyes, his beak pointing upward, every half-hour in daylight, he'd start peeping and I'd come, he'd open that beak to a vast width and I'd warm things to body temperature and stuff them down into that beak until he closed it again.

For months we assumed he was a starling until my brother Jack came up and said he was a grackle. Starlings were introduced into America along with the English sparrow by some Shakespeare buff. Grackles are indigenous and therefore not the overwhelming problem that starlings have become in some places. Both are black-birds, a little smaller than robin size. Grackles have long tails. Coolie was a purple grackle and when he matured, there was a purple sheen to his black head, a greeny iridescence on his black back.

But the main thing about grackles (as well as crows, jays, starlings, etc. etc.) is that they're social creatures. They run in flocks all year long. And being a social creature, Coolie socialized with the society he found in our kitchen. I was without question by far his favorite but whoever came into the kitchen was fair game. He conscientiously fed the two old dogs scraps he'd pick up from the table at dinner. This he seemed to do to bribe them to leave him alone when he chose to hop about the floor picking up crumbs, pecking at toes and pulling shoelaces. Some people he liked better than others and he would fly onto their shoulders or their knees and eat out of their hands. Some were disinterested or afraid of birds landing on them and those he teased without mercy or shame.

Although we had had birds in the kitchen many times before, a canary who sang in Baroque style to join in with the music we were playing, pigeons and parakeets, even a couple of goslings who, however, in a few weeks stunk up the house so badly that we had to move them into the yard. None had been so bright, so brazen, so mischievous as was Coolie the grackle.

Whether Coolie was an exceptionally clever grackle or whether grackles are all that smart, I'm not prepared to say, but the fact was that he could learn anything from one lesson if he chose to and many things he insisted on learning by his own invention.

I knew the flame of the gas stove was a big danger to him. However, I wasn't going to quit cooking in his honor. One day, when he was just learning to fly, I put the pan onto the stove and turned to get the spoon and a second later, I heard "pffft" and smelled burning feathers. I turned back and Coolie was standing near the fire, frightened and confused, his tail shorter by about two inches. "HOT!" I squawked at him, for the first time. After that, he knew that that word meant danger and also, although he worried me often coming close to the flames, he was never again hurt by fire.

Coolie smoked cigarettes with me. He would sit on my shoulder while I smoked and he would peck at my cheek to ask for a drag and so I would put the cigarette there in front of his face and he would put it in his beak for a moment. We did this for months and it was quite a show. But then he developed a little cough and he stopped asking for a drag by pecking at my cheek. I would absent-mindedly put the cigarette there in front of him but he would turn his head away. He had quit smoking and never smoked again.

Once I watched in horror as he jammed his beak into a dog food can with the lid folded back over and the pressure of it held his beak as in a vice. For a second or two he fluttered wildly trying to pull out but the harder he pulled, the tighter it held. So he stopped. And for a second or two he considered. And I saw he was conscious of me there wanting to help. And he was repelled by my help in anything as much as if he were wild. More so, because of the constant consciousness of my wanting to help him. This was one of the lessons he taught me. Spirit and strength are lost when one is dependent, when one is mature.

The one thing he didn't immediately learn about was the dangers of thread. When he was still a fledgling, he tangled his feet in a thread and I grabbed him and held him and cut the thread. When he was mature, it happened again, but he wouldn't let me catch him. Knowing him and his rebellious spirit, it may have been that he got entangled in it simply so that he could complete the act himself, rescue himself from that particular predicament. I was desperate to help him. I could see his feet swelling. I

chased him around the kitchen, even finally with a fish-
net, but it seemed he'd rather lose his feet and most probably also his life than his independence. I left the room
and for what seemed an age sat with my face in my hands,
giving him a chance to do it himself. And when I returned
to the kitchen, the thread was gone and he emanated exhausted defiance.

I realize I've left him with his beak stuck in the dog
food can. All this tale of threads I put in to explain why I
didn't immediately jump to his aid. I had been trained by
him out of such maternal and weakening behavior. What
he did was, he thought for a couple of seconds and then,
clinging to the edge of the can with one foot, shoved the
can's lid further down beside his beak with the other foot,
thus widening the space and releasing his beak.

The way he may have saved the house from burning
down was this. I had put a little pan of coffee on the stove
to warm it up and then, forgetting it, had decided to drive
the three miles to the post office to get the mail. This was
when Stan had left me and was wanting to sell the books
and the art works and I was both clinging to the form we
had made together and realizing that it was dead. It was
definitely not typical behavior on my part to leave a fire
under a pan on the stove and drive away.

It wasn't until I was about a mile from home coming back that I remembered the pan of coffee. I knew the house should be full of smoke, perhaps by then on fire. I remember thinking if it was on fire, I'd have to break the kitchen window to let Coolie out. I drove up and there was no smoke. Dashed in and there was only a faint smell of burn. Rushed into the kitchen and saw the pan tipped so that the gas flame still burned, the now empty and scorched pan was leaning away from the fire onto its wooden handle. The one old dog still left alive was pacing the floor looking worried. Coolie looked both frazzled and smug on the curtain pole across the room. Without doubt he had, knowing I was gone, smelling the fire worsening by the minute, taken the responsibility onto himself to stop it, had flown to the smoking red-hot pan, and with what small strength and weight he had, had brushed against the wooden handle just enough to tip that pan away from the fire.

When I took the trip to Omaha, I knew that when I returned, all the contents of the house, the valuable things that remained, would be removed. So that when I returned from Omaha, I shouldn't have been horrified to see furniture gone, books gone, loved treasures gone, everything valuable gone. It wasn't quite that the house was empty, although the dogs were both dead now. Coolie was still in the kitchen and the kitchen still had all its equipment in it except for some of the beautiful things, but it was functional.

Somehow in the shuffle Stan's mother's old upright piano had found its way into the kitchen. It had a few flaws, a few keys that didn't function, got stuck or whatever. Coolie and I hovered over it, sat on the piano bench and tried to play it, Coolie fluttering about, perching on the top, dancing along the keys, supervising from my shoulder. I didn't know how to play the piano, had learned for a few weeks or months at the age of six and then quit, but trying to play this piano, I could hear that it had a lovely tone. And, knowing that it was essentially a throw-away piano, I decided to take it apart and fix it. It turned out that this was amazingly-to-me possible to do. Especially since there was no one else living in the house and the great ten-foot table that I had made with dreams of poets arguing across it was there beside us, having been too big to go through the door.

The top of the piano was on hinges and so I just tipped it back. Then I saw where I could slide the front cover out. Lovingly, I put it at the far end of the table where it would be out of the way. There were four metal posts, long bolts coming up vertically through a wonderful orderly complex of wires and straps and little hammers and I saw that those bolts were topped simply with thumbscrew nuts. It looked to me like an invitation. Coolie was hopping around with interest. Wide-eyed, I carefully removed the thumbscrews and put them in a little container beside the wooden front. Then I saw that the Action, a large section of the dynamic guts of the piano, was now removable and so, still wide-eyed, I pulled it out and, with Coolie on my shoulder, I laid it down in the middle of the great table.

Symbolism was everywhere. Everything I did, saw, or experienced seemed to resonate with it, seemed to show me from a different angle exactly what I was going through. Knowing practically nothing about pianos but finding beauty in this old instrument, I worked on it with delicate care. As though I was bringing my own self up to where I could make a clear sound, play any note, put together any tune – even now, discarded shambles as I was/felt – more so in that case, because I was listening for cues, for tones to absorb into my gait, my manner, groping for ways to be happy to be what I had suddenly become.

I found a way also how to take out one key at a time and bring that little piece of wood back to its original smooth shape. Jelly had been spilled onto the keys and needed to be scraped off. I started with my Swiss Army knife, worked also with a small cylindrical file, and smoothed and widened wooden holes, trimmed ragged felt with hair shears, checked each key to see if it slid smoothly in its place. Coolie kept me company, danced around me. You would say that I didn't know what I was doing because it was a piano and I didn't know pianos, because it was woodworking and I didn't know wood-working, because it had to do with music and I had not much of an ear for music, but since it was symbolically right and since I found great solace in smoothing and tweaking it back to life, it was just right. It was my transi-tion.

I spent days, weeks, with the parts of that piano lying about on the table, looking at them all for balance and fit and smoothness of movement; and then I felt there was no more that I could do for it and I would put it back to-gether and try it. I was becoming eager to sit and play, to make sounds with those keys and hammers on the wires that were there, the strings, and that delicate structure of the Action. And so I did; I slid the Action down through the vertical bolts and replaced the thumb-screws, put the keys back safe and, as they say, sound. I tried every key and each key sounded good; the sound from each ham-mer had been sharpened. It played, to the best of my hear-ing, well and sounded sweet, very sweet.

Good thing, I thought, that there's no one here but Coolie to hear me. I played folk tunes by ear with one hand but was not satisfied. The piano needed two hands, chords. I found "Für Elise" in the piano bench and figured out how to slowly decipher the lower case. I had learned the upper case when I had learned to play the recorder. And so began the time of learning "Für Elise." Coolie was constantly interested. He had a sort of scholarly manner and that was helpful, as I showed him chords. He loved chords. One day I found him hopping down the keys, trying to hit them hard enough to make a sound. I loved it. He did make some sounds, little light sounds, but it didn't satisfy him and he didn't do it often in my presence.

Always the death of someone is so upsetting that it's hard to remember the life. At one point I went into a deep depression about the loss of my husband and my place in the world. I spent a long time in bed; weeks, I think. And, being in bed, I wasn't there in the kitchen with Coolie. Oh, I'd go in there and have a meal, scatter crumbs for him, be sure he had water, but I wasn't there for him. I was getting rid of my animals because I couldn't be there for them. It was terrible. Some few of them found good homes but some not. I felt horribly guilty. I will let Coolie stand for them all. It was too much suffering. Once one makes an animal dependent, that animal is at the mercy of people always. How many people had mercy for a lot of animals? And here was a grackle. There was no place to release him where he wouldn't very quickly get killed. He spent a lot of time hopping on the ground and cats would catch him. Naturally he would not fear cats as he did not fear dogs. The grackles in town were twice his size and looked like big bullies. He hadn't been raised properly to be let out into grackle society. My only thoughts that pleased me were of driving away and I couldn't figure out how to do that with him. I tried to imagine a curtain, a sort of cage in the back of the car. I never gave any thought to the possibility of actually caging my friend. But then he killed himself by eating the white tips of several kitchen matches and my misery and shame were complete and I was alone.

Coolie's death was a kick-off. But there was a moment between. For some days I slept in the great round chair by the fireplace, not scrubbing off the little white spots Coolie had left on its rim. But, in spite of the fascination of watching a spider live her life on the edge of the windowsill, her amazing patience couching a frightfully quick passion, that life in the great chair wasn't anything that could last and wasn't as comfortable as the car seat put back, so I put the house up for sale and took off alone in the car.

THE CHICKADEE WHO WENT TO THE TOP

He was the only chickadee there at the moment, that moment when I had decided to go up to the top of the ridge above the cabin. "I could use some company," I thought, and of course I had a pocketful of sunflower seeds. So off we went, me stopping every few yards to hold out a handful of seeds. He would come then to my hand and take a seed. At first, he went to a branch and hammered the seed open and ate it, but soon, he would take the seed and tuck it into a cranny in the bark of a tree. I would walk on slowly, knowing that he would catch up to me.

We took the easy route, zigging across through woods to the sloping meadow, up the meadow to its top, then across again to the trail that zagged back across the mountain in the other direction. The chickadee stuck with me. Finally, I wondered if he could have found the way home without me, but that was foolish. He had blazed a trail of sunflower seeds in the trees. He could go easily from one to the other if he kept his cool.

We encountered no other chickadees, no humans either. It was a delight to have his company, but the further I took him from his own territory and his family, the more I worried about him. If he freaked out and left me, would he be all right?

There was a bit of a breeze on the way up, but at the top, the wind was strong. By now, I was so involved with caring for this chickadee that I don't know what I would have done if he hadn't been there. I found a tree that protected us from the wind and we stood, looking out across the canyon below us. "What does he think of this view?" I wondered.

But then, on the wind, a dozen or so migrating Bohemian waxwings touched down and I wished I could give them the rest of the sunflower seeds I had in my pocket. But I feared that the chickadee would be hurt somehow, either by the waxwings themselves or by his own confused departure. I stayed with him under the tree. I didn't give him sunflower seeds in their sight. Somehow, I felt that they would have been interested in eating. I yearned to hold some seeds out to them, but my feeling was that I had chosen the magic I had chosen, and I mustn't endanger it for another that may be more glorious.

We waited until they left and then we went back down, installing sunflower seeds in tree bark all the way. I didn't do that again. Too much responsibility, too much loss of freedom for me. But it was a great occasion.

THE LITTLE OWL

Such a little owl she was, and then there was only that she looked at me. I was out in front of the cabin and the little owl came up to me, that is, she came to a branch very close to me, not within reach, but close. I had never seen such an owl. I had always thought of owls as rather big birds. People told me later that she was a beer can owl.

She deliberately caught my attention. She tipped her head and looked at me. She leaned to one side, looking at me. She looked into my eyes. She tipped in the other direction and leaned forward. She scooted back and forth on her branch, looking at me.

"Oh, you are so adorable!" I said. What else could I say? "Why are you doing this," I wanted to know, and for answer, she paraded on her branch, looking at me. I reached my hand toward her and she flew away. That's all. She was gone.

Everyone who reads fairy tales knows that birds are messengers. And many peoples feel that owls portend a death. "What is the message?" I wondered. So difficult when the messenger doesn't speak English.

Well, yes, my mother, in her nineties, died a few months later. It was no surprise. My life changed. I was just finishing a book, which is always a wrench in the life; I took up with Carlos and found myself spending weekends in town. My concentration was no longer on living up there. Huge changes in my life. But there was that sweet owl face in my mind, looking at me. I figured it must be all right.

TWO TREES

I bought the bay tree about the time I bought the apple trees, two semi-dwarfs, put the little green apple to possibly cover the neighbor's back porch, the Mac I put between the two big windows and started espaliering it. It was great allowing the tree to teach me what I might achieve along that line and during the first few summers, I'd go out every few days and fiddle and adjust the branches. So fun, slowly persuading branches to bend up into a sort of candelabra between the windows. I'd severely cut those branches that wanted to shove me out of the path to the rhubarb.

Yes, and as I said, I bought the bay tree at about the same time, a little sprout, five leaves, three inches tall, in a little pot, so I put it into a bigger pot. Bay trees love sun and water, grow to perhaps twenty-five feet, and if they freeze, they die. In the new pot it grew enthusiastically, lovely scented leaves that I could use in soups and give to friends.

As the years went by, the two apple trees produced apples and the bay tree produced bay leaves. In the summer, I'd put the bay out to stand by the espalier near the back door so that I could cover it if harsh weather came. It was not an easy thing to bring it back in, in the fall. It took two strong people.

In the winter they were together also as the bay peered out the window to gather sun through the growing branches of the espalier. I kept the bay trimmed down to under six feet tall so that it could catch the sun through the window.

This spring, I put the bay out in early May; it had created dozens of bright new leaves and it looked beautiful in the warm May sunshine.

When the storm hit, I had walked to King Soopers on foot and one of the workers there gave me a plastic bag to cover myself and one for a spare to walk home. When I got home, I put the two bags over the bay, top and bottom, and shoved it close under the apple tree for protection.

By this time, the apple had grown upward and outward making a patch of shade over that little pathway. The storm woke me in the middle of the night and I looked out into the storm. In spite of it being the middle of May, there was heavy snow on the branches of the apple tree and they were bent down over the plastic-wrapped bay tree, sheltering it perfectly in a gap between its branches, looking the ultimate image of concern and protection. I thought I couldn't improve on that. It was like knowing that no matter how much a human cared about a baby bird, his own mother would handle him infinitely better, and there they were together by streetlight in a branch-breaking spring snow. That night it got down several degrees below freezing, but the apple plus the plastic bags were making a mini-environment that would be much warmer than that.

At dawn, I went out and gently lightened the load of some of the snow from the apple tree but I waited until it was well above freezing and the snow had gone from crunch and ice crystals to wet globs, then I cleared all the trees. Such a heavy load, trees down all over the city.

When I finally took off the plastic on the following day, the bay was happy and bright. I worked over the apple, making sure it could rise up again, and it did, very satisfactorily. But just where it was touching the top of the bay where I had brought it out to get some sun, I couldn't easily disentangle the two trees, so I left them holding each other for another week or two.

SILLY THE PIG

"When I was a kid," Scott said, "of course I had the job of mucking out the pigpen."

How we got to this point, I cannot say. We were riding on the bus from Boulder to Denver.

"Oh, I've always heard that pigs are smart. Is that so?" I asked.

"Oh, God, yes," he said. "A pig could learn anything. She could bring you your slippers. We had a pig, her name was Silly, because when she was a piglet, she made us laugh with her antics, and that saved her life, because we kept her as a sow. Well, she was strong and healthy, was a good mom, and produced good piglets.

"There was only one problem with her; she could get out of the pen. My dad would bury the fence down a few feet, but she'd get out when the strawberries were ripe and the wind came from that direction. Pigs really like to eat, and when she could smell the strawberry patch, she'd work very hard, get out of the pen and run down to the strawberry patch. A farmer can make a nice bit of money out of a strawberry patch if the pigs don't get into it.

"My dad was an alcoholic," Scot said, "That's why I quit drinking. He was an alcoholic and when he was drinking, which was most of the time, he had a quick temper and so he'd just chase Silly around the strawberry patch and I'd try to help guide her back to the pig pen. Even a nice pig like she was is capable of fighting back and they weigh four hundred pounds, so you always have to be careful with pigs. There was one time, though, that my dad was real drunk and hit her over the head in the strawberry patch with a baseball bat and knocked her out. Then he thought he'd killed her, so he ran for his butcher-ing tools to cut her throat and bleed her out and all, but when he'd found the tools and come back, she had gone to the pig pen and I had let her in."

ALEX AND THE CAT DOOR

Alex was a small, intelligent alley cat. And although he needed to get out and in at his own will, I didn't want to be opening the door for him all the time, so there was a cat door on sale at the pet store and Carlos said he could put it in where the rejected postal slot was. Alex immediately saw what Carlos was doing, he knew it was the cat door of his dreams and he sat purring beside Carlos while he was cutting and fitting. And when he was done, Alex pushed through and went out and pretty soon, he pushed through and came back in again. So that was done.

The door had an outer door made of strips of aluminum curved into a decorative pattern and at the bottom, about an eighteen-inch high piece of frosted plastic. It seemed to me that decorative door should be left open a crack so that Alex could, if he was in a hurry, just slip in and through the cat door.

Alex really didn't like fighting, but at the same time, he felt that it was the only way to relate to tomcats. Since he was a fixed tom, he didn't fight well or hard, and he allowed a small black female cat to come in at night and eat up his cat food. But one day, I came home and as I was putting the key into the lock, I heard a cat fight going on inside the house. And the phone was ringing. I opened the door and left it open because I knew that a strange cat trying to escape the resident cat might have trouble finding the cat door. But a wide-open door would be quite attractive. Left the door open while I grabbed the phone and as I was talking on the phone, watched a handsome Siamese tear out through the open door.

There were other visitors through the cat door, all of them cats. The final straw was an enormous cat who came in several times, showing no interest in Alex's food, but wanted to talk to Alex for hours. "Ow, yow, woo, yawow, ahyo," the lecture went on and on. Alex sat stoically with his eyes half closed. The cat was twice Alex's size and seemed uninterested in me and afraid of nothing. When, after a while, the cat decided to leave for the evening, Alex and I would both sigh with relief and try to return to reality.

By the third evening, when he came in again, I felt that he was here only to enlarge his territory. I couldn't read while he was talking. He was a bore. I had taken up a quilt that I was working on and at one moment, I rose up from my couch, holding the quilt up so it was suddenly a huge form and, walking towards him, roared my best roar. The poor cat hit himself on the edges of the door a few times as he was tearing out of there. I went and closed

the decorative door, looked at Alex who was looking at me, still sitting tall with his eyes slits. I stroked his head. He had maintained his poise. He would have to learn how to get through the double door.

It was a challenge, but he conquered it immediately. Easy enough to get out. Peer out the cat door, through the frosted plastic to see if there are any cats around. Walk out the cat door to the three-inch wide threshold, rise up to jump through the cat-size triangle of twisted aluminum and he's out. Coming back in is the hard part: jump through the triangle and land on the three-inch-wide threshold in such a position that he can come through the cat door. Sometimes he's done it in less than half a second. Usually, he'll take his time and do it right. No other cat nor any other creature has come through that setup, but it's that that has kept us in serene privacy ever since that day that I held up the quilt and roared.

BATS

It was twilight. I went out to bring in the clothes from the clothesline, saw a movement from the front yard where I have a thirty-foot tall maple tree stump holding up my ham radio antenna. There it was again, a bat fluttering around that stump, then two bats. I brought in the clothes and went right out the front door to stand, still as a rock, watching a dozen bats swirling around that tall stump, circling and swirling, seeming to be finding bugs there. Often, they swirled in pairs, the two bats dancing in lovely curls and pirouettes about the stump. Sometimes one would shoot away from the stump, fly in a great arc up over my neighbor's house to the west and down I couldn't tell where, a couple of blocks away, be gone a minute or two and return to swirl again. Others arrived from the east to join the dance. It went on for twenty minutes and then they were gone.

The following evening, I hovered around my windows as the twilight was growing and again saw a bat, went out and stood again to watch them gather and dance around my maple tree stump. Night after night they came, danced gloriously in my front yard for a while, making my day. Soon, I was standing closer to them and they would come to dive at my head. I had no fear of them, knowing they knew where they were going. At first I thought they were saying, "I see you!" but then realized they were catching bugs that had come to dance their own dance above my head.

They came back night after night, for weeks, long enough that the time of their visits became earlier and earlier by the clock to keep coming at the same shade of darkness. One time, the couple next door came, wondering what I was standing there for, and I showed them. She stood by me quietly and he wondered where they slept during the day. I didn't think to tell him that we had installed a bat house fifteen years before in the back alley. He went up to the tree, trying to hear the echolocation sounds, but as I explained, it must have been higher than we could hear. Except for occasional squeaks of chatter among themselves and the occasional quiet hum of a car passing on the quiet street, there seemed to be silence all around those bats.

Weeks later, they started to dwindle down to just a few, then one pair, and then nothing. It had been a great occasion for me. I had hoped they would come back again this year and they have – dancing and whirling again at the predictable time. This year, I watch them, seated, with a glass of wine.

OWL IN THE GARDEN

I like to give the chickens a bit of a treat every day. Often it'll be a half a cheese sandwich. They'll come running and I'll cut it into tiny pieces and they'll chase around to get those crumbs before each other. So that's what I was doing, over by the back porch. I thought I'd lead them to their shed because it seemed it might be about to rain, but strangely, they wouldn't follow me past the fenced-in vegetable patch. I have to fence in the vegetables with a six-foot chickenwire fence or they'll eat up everything.

There, just on the other side of the fence inside the veggie patch, was a small lump and I looked at it closely, and it was a great horned owl, sitting there on the ground, looking up at me. We stared at each other for a while and I got as close as a foot away without causing him to move. He was as small as or smaller than my smallest chicken, Beatrice. He was hard to see, blended in with the March leaf litter, but his really tall horns made of feathers stuck straight up and his great amber eyes looked at me. He was definitely in some unreal zone. I figured he had flown into the wire fence and knocked himself out. Nonetheless, the great amber eyes looked into my eyes and I knew somebody was in there somewhere.

I went to the phone then and called the raptor rescue and they said to toss a towel over him and put him in a box. I had a cat carrier and as I was talking with the raptor guy, I pulled it out of the storage shed which happened to be right there across the path from the owl and at the sight of the cat carrier, he took a few hops away from the fence and I wondered if I had waited too long to catch him. Then he spread his five-foot wingspan and rose over the fence and the sight of those wings set all my chickens screaming. I tried to ignore them, walked slowly between the owl and the outer fence so that he flew again to land on the top of the wire fence. I continued on slowly, slowly moving my arm up and when I touched his breast, he looked down at my hand and I got hold of his leg. He opened his wings again and set the chickens going again. The pull from that one flap was amazing. I got hold of the other leg, pulled him down, wings and all, and folded him up under my arm and held him as I knew how to hold a chicken or any other big bird.

Of course, the cat cage was a complex thing that took two hands to put together, so I walked quietly with the owl under my arm and the cat cage in the other hand to my neighbor's house and my neighbor, with many exclamations and head-shakings, got the cat carrier together and I slipped him in.

That was about it. He sat on my counter, I turned on lights so he'd think it was still daytime and would keep quiet until the raptor lady came and got him and took him away.

They said he was fine, must have flown into the wire fence. They got him to eat, watched him for a few days, and then released him into the prairie.

HIPPOPOTAMUS

Once I was in the zoo watching a hippopotamus swim round and round in his little pool with the grace of a pigeon flying, his huge mass sliding through the water. When he came to one corner of the pool, he would rise up to breathe – snort, gasp, and then sink down and sail on. I went over to that corner to see his face. I was close enough to where he came up so that I could reach out my hand and maybe touch him. He came around and rose up whuffling and saw me there with my hand reaching out and he raised his great head out of the water and slowly opened his mouth. I suppose I could have thrown him a peanut. I imagine now that he expected one but in the face of that vast maw dappled here and there with an occasional monumental square tooth, it seemed it would have been an insult to give him anything less than my arm, so I reached a little farther out and scratched his nose. It was wet, leathery, and hard, and he stayed there a few seconds and I went on scratching his nose. His protruding eyes drooped shut and his monstrous mouth closed very slowly and slowly he sank into the water and stayed there still for a moment and then went back to swimming around and around.